Chrissy stood on the sidewalk in front of the Flatiron Building, staring up at the odd-looking structure, which was shaped like a piece of pie but made of dirty stone. She'd expected *Heart Throb* magazine, where she had an internship for the month, to be located in a tall, glass skyscraper. After boarding an antique elevator which shook and rattled like a tractor-combine on its last legs, Chrissy was relieved to emerge at one end of a short hall. The pink door at the opposite end read, simply, "Heart Throb," in plain black letters. Disappointed, Chrissy opened the door. So far, this wasn't a very glamorous organization.

Instantly she changed her mind as she entered the offices. Rock music pulsed out of invisible speakers, and one entire wall was covered by an enormous reproduction of a *Heart Throb* cover, lit up so that it glowed.

What am I doing in a place like this? she thought helplessly, her mouth hanging open. *I'm an Iowa farm girl, not a chic city socialite!*

Other books in the **SUGAR & SPICE** series:

Janet
Quin-Harkin's
Sugar & Spice

Dream Come True

IVY BOOKS • NEW YORK

To Diane Schwemm

Ivy Books
Published by Ballantine Books

Produced by Butterfield Press, Inc.
133 Fifth Avenue
New York, New York 10003

Library of Congress Catalog Card Number: 88-91126

ISBN: 0-8041-0334-8

Manufactured in the United States of America

First Edition: December 1988

Chapter 1

Chrissy Madden's blue eyes popped open and she sat up abruptly in bed. For a moment she was dazzled by the bright early morning sunlight streaming through the window. *Where am I?* she wondered, her mind still fuzzy and half asleep. She certainly wasn't home on the farm in Iowa. Morning sounds there consisted of roosters crowing and cows mooing. She might be a little groggy but she knew car horns honking when she heard them. Chrissy's hands fumbled around her on the bed, encountering squishy unfamiliar feather pillows and an equally unfamiliar satin comforter. No, she wasn't in her cousin Caroline's bedroom in San Francisco, either—although Caroline certainly did like elegant things, she was way too practical to have satin comforters.

1

Finally, Chrissy realized with a start where she was and snapped fully awake. Leaping to her feet, she gave an energetic bounce, using the bed as a trampoline. "I'm in New York!" she yelled, waving her arms like a windmill. She bounced again, her straight, straw-blond hair swung out in a shiny arc, this time twirling around one hundred and eighty degrees. "Hey, Cara! We're in New York!"

Caroline Kirby made a groaning sound which was muffled by the pillow she'd pulled over her head in response to her cousin's exuberant shout. "I know we're in New York," she said, her tone sleepy and peevish. She moved the pillow away from her face just long enough to peer at the clock and then groaned again. "*Mon Dieu*, Chrissy, it's only six-thirty! You know, we're not on the farm. You don't have to get up at the crack of dawn to slop the hogs or whatever!"

How could Cara be so nonchalant? Chrissy wondered. "It's our very first day in New York City, Caroline Kirby, the Big Apple," she reminded her cousin, pronouncing each word with care. "Aren't you excited?"

"I'll be excited in an hour and a half. Make that *two* hours and a half." Caroline dug back under her pillow like a crab in the sand. "Get back to me then, okay?"

Chrissy shook her head and smiled good-naturedly. She knew how Caroline hated to wake up early. There wasn't much that could rouse her out of bed before eight or preferably nine o'clock in the morning, especially on a weekend. *But today is different*! Chrissy reasoned. She sprang off the bed, landing on the smooth wood floor with a thump of bare feet. "You'll be sorry," she informed Caroline. "You'll be sorry when I'm a bona fide, full-fledged New Yorker a whole two and a half hours before you are!"

Caroline peeked out from under her pillow. "New York will have to wait until I get over my jet lag," she replied with a yawn.

"Jet lag, shmet lag," Chrissy declared. "I'm going out exploring right now. It was too dark to see much by the time we arrived last night."

"What about the spectacular New York skyline?" Caroline reminded her. "You went into such a frenzy when we spotted all the lights across the river, I thought the bus driver was going to turn around and take you back to the airport in New Jersey."

"Seeing the famous skyline just whets my curiosity to go out and explore the city up close. I suppose it doesn't really matter to you. You've been here before," Chrissy said.

Caroline rolled over in bed. "I still think it's exciting, but we've got a whole month to explore the city. Right now I just want to sleep."

Chrissy shrugged, but as she began shuffling through the disordered contents of her well-used suitcase, she gave herself a pinch. It was still hard to believe that she and Caroline were really and truly on their own in New York City, with a whole month of summer fun in front of them. She supposed she understood why the prospect wasn't quite as overwhelming for Caroline as it was for her. After all, Cara had grown up in big, bustling San Francisco, not in a small Iowa town like Danbury, where Chrissy had grown up. And Cara had already traveled in Europe, too. Yes, Caroline had a cool, sophisticated city air—she'd stroll out onto the street and immediately look and act like she belonged. *But what about me?* Chrissy wondered.

She slipped into a pair of baggy lifeguard-orange shorts and a loose yellow T-shirt. She paused in front of an ornate full-length mirror in one corner of the bedroom. Brushing the hair back from her face, Chrissy wrinkled her freckled nose and inspected her image. Her family and friends from home all told her that she'd changed since she first left Danbury, and in some ways she knew they were right. Naturally, she'd gotten older and taller during her two years of living with the Kirbys, but it wasn't just that. She'd also become "citified" to an extent. But inside, especially this morning, Chrissy didn't feel all that different from the way she had the day her plane landed in San Francisco two summers ago.

"Do you think I've changed?" Chrissy asked, turning to look at her cousin in the far bed.

Caroline stopped her tossing for a moment. "How do you mean?"

"Have I changed since you first met me?" Chrissy said.

"Well . . ." Caroline abandoned the idea of

sleep for the time being. She didn't even know where to begin to answer Chrissy's question. Although they were cousins, the two girls had only met when Caroline's mother had invited Chrissy to live with them in California so she could experience a different life-style away from the farm. Suddenly, Caroline grinned.

"What's so funny?" Chrissy demanded.

Caroline shook her head in amusement. "At least you didn't want to go for a ride on the luggage carousel at Newark Airport like you did when you arrived at the airport in San Francisco."

"I told you at the time I was only joking around," Chrissy replied indignantly. "I'm being serious now, Cara. Am I that same bumbling, naive country girl that I was?"

"If you were that same girl, you wouldn't be planning to go to Colorado University in the fall," Caroline reminded her cousin. "You would have grabbed your high school diploma and headed straight for the altar to marry Ben. Just think, you would have been a farmer's wife for the rest of your days."

Chrissy grimaced as she fastened her long hair back in a high ponytail. "Mrs. Ben Hatcher— blech!" she said in a disdainful tone. "Talk about a fate worse than death!"

Quickly, she turned away and busied herself by hunting through her suitcase for her sneakers and a matching pair of socks. Her ex-boyfriend was one of the reasons New York City would be such a welcome change for Chrissy. Danbury had always been a small town but this summer it had seemed smaller than ever, mostly because almost every time she turned a corner Chrissy bumped into Ben and his new girlfriend. She didn't really care about Ben that much anymore. It was her pride, not her heart that still hurt—but her pride sure hurt a lot.

There was no doubt about it, Chrissy thought. Caroline had called her with the New York proposition just in time. It was really a made-to-order situation. Earlier in the summer Caroline's father, a music critic with his own syndicated column, had heard from a good friend who was a jazz musician in New York. Roy Fisher and his ensemble had scheduled a tour in Europe for the month of July and Roy was looking for someone to house-sit his SoHo loft while he was away. So here they were, with a funky apartment and great internships, all thanks to Uncle Richard and Aunt Edith's various connections. On Monday, Chrissy would start as an editorial assistant at *Heart Throb*, a teen magazine, while Caroline would be working with a French interpreter at the United Nations. In the meantime, they had the whole weekend to play!

"I feel like I'm in a dream," Chrissy remarked, making her way to one of the floor-to-ceiling bedroom windows with one sneaker in her hand and the other already on her foot. She peeked out behind the bamboo blind.

"You would be in a dream if you'd settle down

and go back to sleep like me,"Caroline suggested, rolling over and hiding her head under the pillow once again. She'd never make it through a day exploring New York with her overactive cousin if she didn't get a couple more hours' sleep.

But Chrissy was no longer paying attention to her cousin. Her mind was occupied with other things as she gazed at the scene out the window.

Holy Mazoly! And to think that yesterday morning I woke up and looked out my window at the green fields of the farm, she mused, her thoughts turning suddenly serious.

Chrissy loved the farm—it was a part of her. Yet when she boarded the plane yesterday, it had seemed almost a relief to get away. Ben wasn't the only problem she'd left behind. When she had returned to Danbury for summer vacation after the end of her senior year in San Francisco, she had found many changes. Her family's farm, which had been devastated by a tornado the year before, was entirely rebuilt. With the new buildings, the place had an air of prosperity. In reality, however, the insurance payments hadn't covered all the expenses. In order to get a proper fresh start, Chrissy knew her parents had borrowed more money than usual this spring. Chrissy's mother had even taken a job as a cashier at a local store to bring in some extra income. But if the crops weren't good this year . . . Chrissy couldn't bear to think about what might happen.

The house had seemed empty and hollow with her mom working and her three brothers out helping her dad. Chrissy's own prospects for summer employment, outside of performing her usual chores, were not inspiring. But as usual, Chrissy's parents had encouraged her to make the most of a good opportunity. Since the apartment was free and the token salary she'd earn at *Heart Throb* could be put toward her travel and living expenses, cost hadn't really posed a problem.

"Well, if I'm here for real-life experience, I might as well get out there and find some!" Chrissy said aloud, snapping out of her pensive daydream, and returning her concentration to the scene outside the window. Her heart somersaulted. There was the city! At least a part of it. And Chrissy could see that, despite what Caroline might think, she wasn't the only person awake by a long shot. Numerous joggers plugged into Walkman headphones and wearing brightly-striped shorts sprinted by. An elderly lady with a microscopic dog on a jeweled leash paused by a fire hydrant. Other people wandered along the sidewalk with their noses buried in morning newspapers. A street vendor wheeled his umbrella-shaded cart, neatly piled with a rainbow of fresh fruit, down to the corner.

The sight of the fruit made Chrissy's mouth water. She glanced over at her cousin, but only saw a mound of comforter rising and falling with Caroline's deep, even breathing. Well, she didn't have to wait for Caroline to get up to eat breakfast, did she? There was a good chance she would perish from hunger in the meantime. Then Chrissy glanced farther down the narrow, sun-dappled street and noticed a dozen or so people clustered on the sidewalk outside of a tiny cafe. She yanked open one of the windows. Along with the gritty scent of car exhaust came the tantalizing aroma of fresh baking. That decided it. She'd pick up some fresh Italian pastries as a breakfast surprise for Caroline—plus a few extra to tide herself over until her cousin woke up.

Chrissy tiptoed over to the dresser to retrieve the keys to the apartment. After weaving her way through the obstacle course of Grecian columns and enormous pop-art sculptures she faced the elevator. She wasn't even sure if she'd be able to let herself out of the apartment without help from Caroline, but she figured she could give it a try. The loft was on the second floor of a converted warehouse and a renovated freight elevator opened right out into the living room. The elevator could only be summoned by turning the first of three keys in a switch on the wall. Once Chrissy was inside she would have to turn a second key in order to get the elevator to go anywhere, and lastly she'd need the third key to unlock the door on her way back in from the street.

To her surprise and gratification, Chrissy managed the keys successfully and in a few moments she was stepping outside onto the sidewalk. She threw back her head and took a deep, experimental breath. It sure didn't smell like Iowa—that fresh hay, damp earth, farm animal scent Chrissy loved so much—but it did smell exciting.

In a few moments, Chrissy reached the cafe that smelled so good. She paused outside the door. The people who'd been gathered on the sidewalk when she'd looked from the loft window were now milling around inside the cafe. The place was packed! She'd probably have to wait on line for half an hour, just for a couple of pastries. But that was the city for you, Chrissy thought, recalling the bustling delicatessens and bakeries in San Francisco.

Then Chrissy spotted the cameras and lights. The *movie* cameras and lights. Chrissy gulped, a thrill running down her spine. They were making a movie right here, right down the street from where she and Caroline were living! Chrissy didn't think twice. This was her big chance! She was sure she was about to be discovered. Maybe they'd even recruit her right on the spot to be an extra!

Wait till everyone back in Iowa goes to the local theater and sees my face up on the screen! Chrissy thought as she pulled the door open eagerly, jangling the bells that hung from the inside handle.

Immediately, a hush fell over the cafe. She hadn't taken two steps past the entrance when a bald man in leather pants and a leather tie gripped her arm, spun her around, and curtly pointed at the "Closed" sign hanging on the door. "Can't you read, lady?"

"But I saw your film equipment from outside and I thought you might like another extra," she stammered, glancing up at him hopefully. "You don't even have to pay me."

A round of laughter echoed through the cafe.

"Hey, Rocco, I'm an actress, not a cook. These pastries are burning," a voice said from the back. "Let's just do another take."

Chrissy strained her neck to see who was speaking. *Could it be someone famous?* she wondered. But before she could catch even the tiniest glimpse, she felt Rocco propelling her back out onto the sidewalk.

"You've just lost yourself some free publicity for your dumb movie," Chrissy shouted, but the door had already swung shut behind Rocco with a pronounced *bang*.

Chrissy shrugged her shoulders and, taking a last longing look through the windows of the cafe, headed back in the direction of the apartment. *So much for being discovered,* she thought cheerfully. *So much for the pastries!*

The morning sun had risen higher and it was already starting to get hot. There really wasn't a minute to lose, Chrissy decided as she stood in line at the fruit vendor, no matter how much Caroline might want to sleep in. There was a whole new city full of people, shops, parks, and museums to discover! *And someone might even be filming another movie somewhere,* she thought to herself with a grin.

Chapter 2

Caroline sat up in bed, stretching her arms lazily. Had she been dreaming or had Chrissy woken up at an indecently early hour and whipped out of the apartment like an Iowa tornado, all the while shouting something about "discovering New York City"? Caroline rubbed her eyes and looked around the bedroom. No, she hadn't been dreaming. The sheets and comforter were shoved in a tangled heap at the foot of her cousin's bed and the Iowa State football jersey Chrissy wore as a nightgown was draped over the clock on the night table as if she'd undressed in mid-flight.

With two fingers Caroline reached over and gingerly lifted the crumpled jersey from the clock, flinging it onto Chrissy's bed. At the sight of the time, she flopped back in her own bed with a wide yawn. Just because Chrissy was a lunatic didn't mean she couldn't sleep late on Saturday morning like a sensible person.

Caroline rolled over, pulling the goose down pillow across her face to block out the sunlight. She lay quietly for a few minutes only to discover that she couldn't doze off again. *Chrissy's enthusiasm must be catching*, she thought to herself with an amused grin. *It's kind of embarrassing to think that I'm as gung ho as Chrissy!* But here she was, wide awake and ready to join her cousin in exploring the city.

Caroline hopped out of bed and began neatly tucking in her sheets and comforter and fluffing up the pillows. She supposed worse things could happen to her than catching some of Chrissy's enthusiasm.

As outrageous as her behavior often was, Chrissy's intentions were always good and there was no denying that she brought life and sunshine into everything she did. She was open, generous, and down-to-earth. Caroline thought it might have something to do with the fact that Chrissy had grown up in a small town as part of a large, boisterous family. She smiled as a picture of Chrissy's three blond, freckly brothers emerged in her mind. But then another face intruded—the dark, handsome face of Luke Masterson, Caroline's boyfriend and the Maddens' neighbor in Iowa.

My boyfriend . . . Make that my ex-boyfriend! Caroline smoothed her hand across the comforter, a quiet sigh escaping her. *Here I go again,* she reflected, irritably. *I can't think about anything these days without having my thoughts end up with Luke!*

And he wasn't worth thinking about—that's what Caroline had decided only a few weeks earlier, when she and Luke had last talked on the phone. It had been clear from the start, really, that they had nothing in common. They lived in two different worlds: she was a city girl and he was a country boy. *How had their romance managed to last this long?* Caroline wondered. She and Luke had been a steady couple ever since she had met him on a vacation to Danbury during her junior year. For a long time, the miles between them had seemed bearable, so long as they could look forward to being together.

I should have known it was doomed to fall apart eventually, Caroline told herself. She couldn't even count the number of times she'd tried to console herself with that thought since the fateful phone call when Luke had admitted that he was seeing another girl. Caroline would rather not remember that she and Luke had shared something wonderful, that she had never cared so much for any boy before. She didn't like to think back to the time they met, how at first they'd bickered—Luke thought Caroline was a snob and she thought he was a hick. Then Luke had taken her for a ride in the tiny, rickety old plane he used on his crop-dusting job and they'd gotten caught in a freak spring blizzard. They'd only survived by breaking into an abandoned farmhouse and making a small campfire to keep warm. Caroline recalled Luke's arm around her, the sparkle of firelight in his eyes, and the wonderful contented sensation that she'd felt when they'd kissed for the first time.

Now she clenched her teeth as she gave one of the pillows a swat. Remembering that moment and other magical times she'd had with Luke was making her miss him when she wanted to be mad at him. Not only was he seeing someone else— that same awful Tammy Laudenschlager who'd tried to break up Chrissy's relationship with Ben a year ago—but Luke had made plans for the future that clearly didn't include Caroline. After promising each other that they'd find a way to be together after they graduated from high school, he'd decided not to go to Colorado University with her. Instead, he was going to study to be a pilot at the Air Force Academy in Fort Collins, Colorado, several hours from the university.

"It's over, Cara," she said aloud. "Luke Masterson is history."

But here she was still daydreaming about their first kiss. It was definitely time to shape up. She'd already spent too much of her last free summer before college moping over Luke. She and Chrissy had both resolved to put Luke and Ben out of their minds and move on to bigger and better things—and New York City was their big chance. Caroline didn't think Chrissy would have too tough a time keeping her resolution. Chrissy

tended to bounce back from misfortunes like a
brand-new tennis ball, and besides, she and Ben
had been drifting apart for a long time before
they finally called it quits. Caroline and Luke
were another story altogether.

At that moment Chrissy burst back into the
bedroom, the smile on her face bright enough to
light up the Empire State Building. "Cara, you'll
never believe what just happened to me!" she
announced, flinging herself onto her cousin's
newly made bed and scattering the linens until it
was as much of a mess as her own unmade bed.

"Oh, yes I will," Caroline said dryly.

She shook her head and smiled at her cousin.
Trust Chrissy to have an adventure during her
first hour in New York! "Don't tell me, Chrissy,"
she said, a teasing note in her voice. "You got
scooped up by a street sweeper and almost ended
up in the city trash. No, wait a minute—you
couldn't get the keys to work downstairs so you
had to shinny up the elevator shaft."

Chrissy stuck her tongue out at Caroline. "No,
no, no. Something glamorous, something thrill-
ing, something that could only happen in New
York City!" Without pausing for breath Chrissy
rattled off her story about the movie being filmed
at the cafe down the street.

Caroline raised one dark-blond eyebrow.
"You're right," she admitted. "I don't believe
you."

Chrissy jumped to her feet, indignant. "Just
look out the window, Cara! See for yourself!"

"I was just kidding." Caroline waved at Chrissy with both hands to calm her down. "My motto is, if it could happen to anyone, it'll happen to you. So I believe you, I believe you!"

Chrissy grinned, mollified. "See what you miss by sleeping half the day away?" she said, crossing her arms triumphantly. "I've already encountered famous film stars and directors and producers."

"Yes," Caroline countered, "but at this rate you'll be ready for bed at eight o'clock tonight while I'll still be fresh as a daisy. And nighttime is when things really happen around here. This is the city that never sleeps, remember?"

Chrissy wasn't daunted. "These are the legs that led the Danbury High School cheerleading squad through about a million leaps and jumps," she reminded Caroline, extending one of the legs as evidence. "I can walk all day and dance all night!"

While Caroline took a quick shower, Chrissy started in on the fresh fruit she'd bought from the street vendor. By the time Caroline returned, running a comb through her wet shoulder-length hair, Chrissy had polished off a banana, a peach, and a fair-sized bunch of seedless grapes. "I'm still starving!" Chrissy complained to her cousin. "It's going to take more than this to keep me going today."

Caroline paused in the act of slipping into a short blue skirt and a matching sleeveless knit top. "Chrissy, with your appetite, you'll never be full. It's just a matter of time before you eat so much your stomach will burst."

Chrissy pressed her lips together in mock annoyance and Caroline knew a motherly lecture was coming her way. "Now, Caroline," Chrissy said, wagging a finger at her. "If you ate a big balanced breakfast every morning like me you'd feel great all day! As it is, I know you. You'll eat one peach and in a couple of hours you'll be begging to take a taxi home. We'll see who tires out first!"

Caroline finished dressing and the two girls headed for the elevator in the living room, dodging the life-sized sculptures along the way. As Caroline started to turn the key in the switch to call the elevator, something occurred to her. She pivoted around to look at Chrissy. "Where are we going, anyway?" she asked. "What are we doing today?"

Chrissy stared at Caroline, uncomprehending. "What do you mean, where are we going? We're going outside. We're going to see New York."

"New York's a pretty big place," Caroline reminded her cousin. "I mean, we can't just 'see' it. We need a plan, an itinerary."

Chrissy considered this. "Hmm. Be right back!"

While Chrissy bolted back into the bedroom, Caroline flopped down on one of the low, unstructured couches scattered around the living area. She felt like she was on some strange space-age park bench: Instead of looking up at trees she was surrounded by a grove of free-form sculptures.

Chrissy returned just seconds later waving a brand-new paperback book entitled *150 Must-See New York City Sights*. Caroline felt weak just at the thought of it. "*Mon Dieu,* Chrissy, don't even tell me. You want to see all one hundred and fifty before lunch!"

Chrissy sat down next to Caroline and opened the book to the first page in a businesslike manner. "Of course not, silly. Even *I'm* not that much of a dumb tourist. This is just to help us make our 'itinerary.'" Chrissy pronounced the word with an exaggerated imitation of Caroline's sophisticated accent. Caroline swatted her on the shoulder. "We'll make a list of our priorities, the places we want to go and the things we want to do first, okay?"

"Okay," Caroline agreed. "That sounds like a good idea."

"You start," Chrissy encouraged her.

Caroline thought for a moment, her head tilted to one side and her fine blond hair swinging across her face. "Well, I've really been looking forward to going to the Met. That would probably be my first choice."

"The Mets?" Chrissy's face brightened. "Yeah, they have a great team this year. Dwight Gooden and Darryl Strawberry—"

"Not the Mets, the *Met,*" Caroline corrected Chrissy. "As in the Metropolitan Museum of Art."

"Oh." Chrissy couldn't hide her disappointment. "That sounds . . . fun. But, um, wouldn't you rather see a ball game? One of the New York teams is sure to be playing at home this afternoon—"

"Definitely not. We didn't come all this way just to see a baseball game. We could have done that in California," Caroline objected.

Chrissy shrugged cheerfully. "Well, maybe we could agree on something else. How about exploring Central Park? According to my book there's a zoo there and also a big lake, right in the middle. We could rent a rowboat and paddle around!"

Caroline looked doubtful. "I was thinking more along the lines of exploring the Fifth Avenue shops," she confessed. "The park will be so crowded on a warm day like this. I hear it gets as bad as the state beaches on Long Island."

Chrissy shrugged again, tossing her book down. "Jeepers, Caroline, the whole *city* will be crowded," she pointed out. "That's part of the fun, isn't it? That's why we're here, right? To be part of the action!" Chrissy jumped to her feet. "C'mon! Forget this itinerary business. My way's better. Let's just *go!*"

With that she pulled Caroline up from the couch and into the waiting elevator.

Chapter 3

A few minutes later, the girls were standing on the sidewalk in front of Roy Fisher's building, studying the bus and subway map Caroline had thought to grab on their way out. A rainbow of crooked, color-coded lines crisscrossed the page.

Chrissy whistled. "If you can make any sense out of that, Cara, you're even smarter than I thought."

Caroline eyed the diagram for a moment. Then, shading her eyes with one hand, she looked down the street first to the east and then to the west. On the elevator ride down, the cousins had reached a compromise, deciding to spend the morning uptown checking out the museum *and* the park. They'd return to their new neighborhood in the afternoon to take themselves on a walking tour of SoHo and Greenwich Village.

"Well," Caroline said, "according to the directions Mr. Fisher left us, we can pick up the green line subway three blocks that way or an uptown bus one block in the other direction. The subway is faster and they cost the same. What do you say?"

Chrissy was already bouncing down the sidewalk, her ponytail swinging with a life of its own. "The subway, naturally! I've never ridden one."

She wasn't bouncing quite so energetically, however, after they left the bright, busy sidewalk to walk down the dark stairs to the subway platform. Carefully placing her token in the slot, Chrissy pushed through the turnstile. Then she froze. A booming noise, far off at first, filled the underground station. The sound, echoing off the stone walls and shaking the cement under their feet, grew louder and louder. All of a sudden headlights burst into view as the train rounded a turn in the tunnel on its approach to the station.

Caroline had stepped calmly to the edge of the platform to wait with the other passengers, leaving Chrissy behind. Now Chrissy dashed forward and gripped her cousin's arm. Then, with all her might, she yanked Caroline back against the wall.

"Chrissy, what on earth are you doing?" Caroline gasped.

"Saving your life, what do you think?" Chrissy's eyes were wide and she was panting slightly. Just then the subway roared into the station, screeching to a stop alongside the platform. The doors whipped open and Caroline started toward the train, but Chrissy held back.

"I don't think I want to ride the subway after all," she said in a small voice.

"Oh, yes you do!" This time it was Caroline who grabbed Chrissy, hauling her onto the train only seconds before the doors slid shut again with a smack.

The train was only half full as it lurched forward and the cousins collapsed in two adjacent seats. Chrissy started to laugh. She felt safer already, now that she was securely on board and in motion. "Sorry I freaked out," she whispered to Caroline. Her curious spirit quickly reasserted itself and she began scanning the subway car, studying the other occupants and reading the poster advertisements above the grimy windows. "It's just that this is a lot different from riding the cable cars in San Francisco!"

Caroline nodded. Her own heart was thumping a little faster than usual. Chrissy wasn't the only one the subway had taken somewhat by surprise. It *was* a lot different from San Francisco, even Caroline had to admit.

They got off the train on the Upper East Side and walked a few blocks west in the direction of Central Park. Even though it wasn't far, it took the two girls half an hour to reach the museum. Every few steps Chrissy stopped in her tracks to crane her neck up at the buildings, or stare at the people hurrying by on the sidewalk, or fumble in her pocket for some change to give to a street person holding a hat out for money. Finally they found themselves in front of the enormous Metropolitan Museum of Art. Colorful banners announced special exhibits, which caused Caroline's eyes to light up with anticipation. She squeezed Chrissy's arm excitedly. Chrissy looked skeptical. "I still think we should have gone to a baseball game!" she muttered under her breath.

"Oh, c'mon, Chrissy," Caroline said briskly. "You're in New York to get *culture*, and I don't think you'd find it at Yankee Stadium."

"Culture, shmulture," Chrissy said, but this time Caroline didn't hear her. She was three steps ahead of Chrissy, practically sprinting up the stairs to the museum entrance. Once inside, she picked up a brochure at the information desk and began checking the locations of the exhibits that interested her. "Of course we have to walk through the special Georgia O'Keeffe show, and the modern paintings and sculptures are a must. They also have a wonderful Impressionist collection here."

Chrissy was reading over Caroline's shoulder. "The Egyptian room!" she shrieked. "Oh, boy, we have to go there! Do you suppose they have mummies?"

Caroline looked around, embarrassed in case anyone should have overhead Chrissy's exclamation. "The Egyptian room is for kids, Chrissy," she said, lowering her voice in the hope that Chrissy would follow suit.

But Chrissy held her ground. "I gave up the Mets for the Met, Cara," she reminded her cousin. "The least you can do is let me have some fun with the mummies! Fair is fair."

"You're right." Caroline refolded the brochure with a sigh of defeat. Trying to make Chrissy a cultured person had always been an uphill battle; it would take more than a change in mere location to alter that. "But we'll do the Egyptian room last. It's the farthest from this point."

To both Caroline's and Chrissy's surprise, Chrissy liked all the exhibits, especially the Impressionist paintings. She spent more time than Caroline, stepping back and fully absorbing the subtle blending of color in each one. It was Caroline who ended up getting antsy as Chrissy stood spellbound in front of a Pissarro for what seemed like half an hour. Chrissy's blue eyes had grown dreamy. "It looks just like Iowa, Cara," she breathed rapturously. "Early in the summer when the meadow flowers are blooming. That's exactly what it looks like when the sun's in your eyes and you squint a little. Oh, I can almost smell the wild roses!"

"Well, I can almost smell the embalming fluid," Caroline declared impatiently, steering Chrissy away from the Pissarro. "What do you say, King Tut and Company and then lunch?"

After the museum, Chrissy and Caroline wandered into nearby Central Park. On the streets, the midday sun had become unbearably hot, but the park was green and cool and breezy, just right for a stroll. The cousins took their time; there was so much to see. Chrissy waved to the drivers of the horse-drawn carriages and clucked to the horses. She struck up conversations by the dozen—something Caroline would never dare to do in a city full of strangers. She chattered with the vendor at the hot-dog stand, the dreadlocked members of a sidewalk reggae band, a woman pushing triplets in a three-tiered baby carriage, and the man who sold her a flattened penny printed with the image of the Empire State Building.

"The Empire State Building. That's it!" Chrissy declared suddenly, pointing to the sky as she and Caroline emerged from the south end of the park onto Fifth Avenue to do some window-shopping.

"Sure is," Caroline replied, recognizing the landmark skyscraper half a mile down Fifth Avenue.

Chrissy gave an excited hop, her sneakers squeaking. "Come on, Cara, let's go! I want to go up to the top! I bet we could see clear to Iowa on a day like this!" She began running down Fifth Avenue, dodging the people in her way. Caroline followed more slowly, catching up to her cousin at the next traffic light.

"Chrissy, I thought we were going to go window-shopping," she said. "All the good stores are on this stretch of Fifth Avenue."

"But we can't afford anything, anyway," Chrissy protested.

"That doesn't matter." Caroline looked at the excited glow on her cousin's face, and sighed. She could come back some other time to go window-shopping. "You're right. Let's go to the top of the Empire State Building," she conceded, hurrying across the street as the light turned green.

Caroline did end up being glad she'd let Chrissy have her way when they stood together on the Empire State Building observation deck. The view from almost one hundred stories in the air was breathtaking.

First the cousins faced north. They were eye level with the skyscrapers of midtown, and beyond midtown, far below them, lay the emerald-green ocean of Central Park.

"Holy mazoly," Chrissy breathed. "We were way down there less than an hour ago, underneath all those trees!"

Crossing to the other side of the observation deck, they gazed at the twin towers of the World Trade Center at the southernmost tip of Manhattan Island. The East and Hudson Rivers converged, sparkling blue in the sun and dotted with boats of all shapes and sizes. Caroline was awestruck in spite of herself. San Francisco was certainly spectacular, but New York was bigger and bolder than any other place she'd been.

Just as Caroline was losing herself dreamily in the clouds, Chrissy jolted her back to her senses. "Say cheese, Cara!" Chrissy ordered.

Caroline turned away from the vista and

blinked. Her cousin was prancing around her, scanning her through the viewer of her camera, trying to get the best angle.

Caroline put a hand to her face in exasperation. The other sightseers nearby were staring and smiling at Chrissy's antics. "Chrissy, do you have to make such a fuss? Just take the picture already!"

Chrissy quickly clicked the button. Then before Caroline had a chance to grab the camera and put an end to the photo session, she turned to a man standing a few feet away. "Excuse me, sir? Would you please take a picture of me and my cousin?" Chrissy asked in her most polite, appealing manner.

The man looked at Chrissy with a blank expression on his face. Chrissy tried again, but the man simply shrugged his shoulders.

"*No hablo inglés.*"

Now Chrissy gave the man a blank expression of her own.

"I think that means he doesn't speak English," Caroline remarked. She began to walk away, hoping that Chrissy would forget about the picture. A moment later, however, she saw her cousin demonstrating in a rather confused sign language what she wanted the man to do. After a few moments, a glimmer of understanding appeared in his eyes.

Darn, Caroline thought as Chrissy pulled her over to be in the picture. But when Chrissy put an arm around her shoulders and beamed at the obliging stranger aiming the camera, Caroline's expression softened and she managed a heartfelt smile. She had a feeling the photograph would be one she'd cherish forever.

It was past three o'clock by the time Chrissy and Caroline caught another bus down to Greenwich Village. A late lunch at an outdoor cafe fortified them for an hour of shopping among the funky Village clothing boutiques. They concluded what by now seemed like an endless day by visiting a few art galleries in SoHo, which fascinated Caroline, but had Chrissy shaking her head at the crazy things that people called art.

"If I take one more step, I'll drop," Caroline moaned as they left their last gallery at six o'clock. She leaned over to squeeze the big toe of her left foot through her shoe.

"You should have worn sneakers like me," Chrissy said. "But I've gotta confess I'm just about dead myself."

The sun was still high, filtering hazily through the leafy branches of the trees that lined the street every few yards. The trees were a refreshing sight against all the concrete of the city. Chrissy and Caroline walked very slowly in the direction of their apartment, wishing it were just a little further away so they could justify taking a taxi. Inside the loft they sprawled on the sofas, lifeless.

"I'll never walk again," Caroline declared with weary conviction.

"What about dancing all night? You know, 'the city that never sleeps,' and all that?" Chrissy asked mischievously.

Caroline tossed a leopard-print cushion at her. "Okay, okay. Don't rub it in. I admit it—I over-estimated myself. But seriously, why don't we save the nightclubs for another time?"

Chrissy kicked off her sneakers and put her feet up on the couch. "It's still early, though. We can't call it quits at six-thirty on our first day in New York!"

"Maybe you're right," Caroline admitted. "Well, what do you have in mind? Nothing's an option that involves motion of any sort. Sitting is about all I'm capable of at this point."

"Let's see . . ." Chrissy reached for her book of *150 Must-See New York City Sights* and turned to the "Nightlife" chapter. "How about Radio City Music Hall? I've heard they have great shows there. The Rockettes and all. When my Uncle Homer was in New Jersey for a milk pasteurizers' convention a few years ago they came up to the city for the day and—"

"Um, Chrissy, I'm not really in the mood for Radio City tonight," Caroline said. "That's a little too touristy for me. How about the opera at Lincoln Center?"

Chrissy hooted. "You've *got* to be kidding, Cara! Remember the last time—the first and last time—I went to the opera, with you and Aunt Edith and Uncle Richard in San Francisco?"

Caroline remembered only too well. Chrissy

had yawned conspicuously throughout the most dramatic solos and arias, but worse than her yawning was her *talking*. She'd expressed her inexperienced opinion of the performers and the performance frequently and loudly, to the amusement of a few people sitting nearby and the annoyance of many others. "Scratch the opera," Caroline said quickly. "But Radio City Music Hall . . . I don't know. . . ."

The two girls scowled at each other for a few seconds and then both burst out laughing. "This is the exact same argument we started out the day with! Why don't we just scratch *everything*," Chrissy suggested. She slumped down even lower on the sofa, her eyelids drooping. "You were right this morning, Cara. We don't have to see and do everything in one day. And it's so comfortable right here. . . ."

Caroline was relieved. It would be delicious just to relax. "That's the best idea you've had all day," she told Chrissy, yawning. "But what are we going to do about supper? I'm exhausted, but I'm also starving. And there's nothing in the fridge. We forgot to go food shopping."

Chrissy was silent for a minute and then her blue eyes lit up. "I know! There's a video store just down the street. We could rent a few movies and order Chinese food to be delivered. It would be just like an evening in San Francisco!"

All of a sudden Caroline realized that she was more than a little homesick. Chinese food and movies on Mr. Fisher's VCR would be comforting after the novelty of New York City. She smiled at her cousin. Sometimes Chrissy was a downright genius. "You pick up the movies and I'll find a restaurant in the Yellow Pages. Deal?"

Chrissy was already sticking her feet back in her sneakers. "Deal!" she affirmed.

Chapter 4

"I suppose the other summer interns at *Heart Throb* and the United Nations will be college kids, don't you think, Cara?"

Two mornings later, Chrissy and Caroline were standing in front of one of the floor-to-ceiling mirrors in the loft's cavernous bathroom, putting the finishing touches on their makeup before their first day of work. At Chrissy's casual question, the knot in Caroline's stomach grew even tighter, so tight in fact that she was sure even Houdini would have had trouble untying it. Secretly, she'd been worried about the same thing as Chrissy. What if she were the youngest person in her department at the U.N.? All the sophisticated college students would look down on her.

Caroline knew from experience, though, that

no one had to *know* she was nervous and insecure. She looked critically at her reflection. Her
petal-pink linen suit and silk blouse, the slim
leather briefcase her parents had given her
before she left San Francisco, a pearl necklace
and matching solitaire earrings, all added up at
least to a professional, confident appearance.
And appearing confident was a small step toward
feeling confident—Caroline knew that from experience, too.

She glanced at Chrissy, who was buckling a
wide leather belt around her khaki-colored,
safari-style dress. *Why is she worried?* Caroline
wondered. *She won't be intimidated by being the
youngest person at the magazine. She'll fit right
in from moment one. I wish it were that easy for
me.* But, of course, it wasn't.

"Okay, are you sure you know where you're
going?" Caroline asked Chrissy as they hurried
down the bustling sidewalk in the direction of the
subway.

Chrissy laughed at Caroline's anxious tone. "I
get off at the Twenty-third Street stop and walk
east," she said, sounding like a child repeating
her school lesson. "I can't miss the Flatiron
Building—it's at the intersection of Twenty-third,
Broadway, and Fifth Avenue. We practiced all
this yesterday, Cara, remember?"

"I know, I know!" The dress rehearsal had been
Caroline's idea. They had determined the routes
to their jobs and then practiced to find out
approximately how long it would take to get to

the U.N. and to the *Heart Throb* offices. "I just wouldn't want you to be late on your first day of work, that's all."

"Thanks, Cuz," Chrissy said affectionately.

This time when they entered the subway station, Chrissy popped in her token and stepped boldly up to the platform like a pro. There was quite a mob of commuters already waiting and the two girls were lucky to squeeze onto the next uptown train. Caroline did not like being pressed up against the bodies of total strangers, but overcrowded trains seemed to be an unavoidable fact of New York City life. She and Chrissy had already discovered that the buses were a lot slower and no less crowded.

Chrissy's stop came first. The two girls said a hurried goodbye before the door of the subway slammed shut between them. Caroline watched Chrissy through the window until the train rounded a bend, roaring on to the next stop. She gulped. She was really on her own now. In just a few minutes it would be her turn to disembark and transfer to the crosstown bus that would drop her off near the U.N.

All too soon Caroline was standing on the sidewalk in front of the United Nations building. It was *huge*. Caroline's pulse was racing and despite the warm morning, she grew cold right down to her toes. Taking a deep breath, Caroline joined the flood of people moving as one up the long, wide set of stairs.

Inside, Caroline's nervousness gave way to

excitement. She was surrounded by important-looking men and women, most dressed in conservative American business suits, but a few in exotic clothing from their native countries. The babble of voices was an intoxicating mixture of languages. Caroline was thrilled to find herself in an elevator to the fifth floor with three handsome young men chatting in French. She studied them out of the corner of her eye and listened to their conversation, pleased that she could understand so much. The way the men were talking, Caroline figured they must have very responsible positions at the U.N., and she wondered if one of them was J. Roche, the interpreter who would be her boss.

Once off the elevator, though, the Frenchmen headed one way while Caroline, following the signs on the wall, went in another. She located the door she was looking for and checked her watch. It was 8:58—she was right on time. She knocked lightly and waited. When there was no answer she turned the door handle and peeked in. She had expected a plush, quiet office in keeping with the elegant decor of the hall. Instead, she entered a large open room, crammed with desks, chairs, screens denoting semi-private cubicles, and a vast array of audio visual equipment. A number of people were already at work, headphones on and fingers busy at computer keyboards. Caroline clutched the handle of her briefcase more tightly.

Before Caroline could step forward and tap the

nearest shoulder to ask for assistance, the door to an inner office swung open and a tall middle-aged woman wearing a very elegant silk suit approached her. The woman smiled broadly and held out one perfectly manicured hand.

"You must be Caroline Kirby. I'm Juliet Roche. I'm so pleased to meet you."

Caroline smiled back, her knees melting with relief. Despite her cool, polished European appearance, Juliet Roche's expression was far from frosty. Juliet Roche might not be the gorgeous young Frenchman she'd been hoping for, but Caroline felt instantly that she would enjoy working with her.

"Hello," Caroline said, shaking the older woman's hand. "It's nice to meet you, Madame . . . Mademoiselle . . ."

She brushed off Caroline's formality with a light wave. "Please call me Juliet."

Caroline tried her hardest to memorize the names of the other staff members as Juliet whirled her through the room tossing off introductions, but by the time the last hand had been shaken she realized she'd already forgotten every single one. Just as Chrissy had predicted, though, the other summer interns were college students. There were two boys and three other girls, and Caroline thought they looked a lot older than she did. They just had that collegiate air about them. And not only that, the other interns seemed to be working without much supervision, as if they already knew exactly what

to do. *They've probably been at the U.N. since
their colleges let out in late May or early June,*
Caroline thought unhappily. *Here it is July
already and I'm just starting.* As the youngest
intern and the only one in training, Caroline was
sure she would stand out like a sore thumb.

Don't psyche yourself out, Caroline lectured
herself silently as she followed Juliet into her
office. *I might be younger than they are, but I
learn fast and I'm already pretty fluent in French.
There's really nothing to worry about.* But she
wasn't convinced.

Juliet spent almost an hour explaining the ins
and outs of the translators' various responsibili-
ties. Like the other interns, for the most part
Caroline would be transcribing tapes from the
U.N. sessions from French into English. In addition, Juliet promised that Caroline would have a
chance to sit in the booth during an actual session
or two and watch Juliet, an expert simultaneous
translator, at work.

"I hope you'll enjoy working at the U.N.," Juliet
said. "I think our other summer interns are finding it to be a very good experience so far."

"Oh, I know I'll like it!" Caroline exclaimed, her
eyes glowing. "And I really appreciate your giving me the internship at such late notice."

Juliet smiled. "From what I've heard about you
through Miranda Harrington, I think you'll be an
excellent translator."

Caroline didn't know what to say. She barely
knew Miranda Harrington, but she was the friend

of her mother who had recommended her for the internship. *I only hope I can live up to Juliet's expectations*, she thought.

"Are you interested in studying international relations in college?" Juliet asked.

"I hadn't thought about it," Caroline confessed. "I've been looking through the Colorado University course catalogue wondering what to take in the fall, but there's so much to choose from I don't know how I'll ever decide."

"Well, maybe this internship will help you find a direction." Juliet smiled as she pushed her chair back from the broad chrome desk. "Are you ready for the grand tour?"

Juliet pointed out the practical things first: the nearest bathroom and staff cafeteria. Then she led Caroline through the library, where row upon row of computer terminals nearly outnumbered the rows of books.

They reentered the wide hall, heading now for the spacious auditorium where the General Assembly met. "This is it," Juliet said simply.

It was empty; the assembly was not in session, but even unoccupied the huge, echoing room seemed to pulse with a sort of presence. Caroline held her breath as she stepped through a set of double doors. In this very room decisions were made that affected the whole world. "It looks just like it does on TV and in the pictures in magazines!" she said in a low, awed voice. "Can I see where you sit when you're translating?"

"Of course." Juliet led her to an inconspicuous

door, behind which was an elevator which traveled with an almost inaudible hum up one level. Together they entered a glass-fronted booth looking down on the semicircle of chairs below. "The French delegation sits there." Juliet pointed. "Each member wears a small set of headphones through which he or she hears the discussion translated as it is taking place. That way they don't miss anything and they can reply right away."

Caroline shook her head, her fair hair swinging from side to side with the motion. "I don't know how you do it," she declared admiringly. "If I hear something spoken in French I have to stop and think for a minute before I even attempt a translation. And that's taking it one sentence at a time!"

"That's why we're starting you out transcribing recordings, not doing this," Juliet told Caroline. "The U.N. delegates don't give the translators any concessions. They talk very fast and they don't pause between statements. But I assure you, simultaneous translation is not magic. Translators must pay very close attention and think quickly, but for the most part the skill comes from a lot of practice and experience."

The two sat for a few moments in silence. Caroline stared out over the expanse of the auditorium. With the help of her imagination, she could hear the raised voices of a debate. Arms control, the Middle East, Central America, international terrorism, human rights . . . Any of these could be the subject of controversial, policy-forming discussion. Maybe her one-month internship with Juliet was just the beginning of something. Maybe some day she would be sitting down there as an American delegate!

Before Caroline could daydream herself right on up into the chair of the president of the General Assembly, Juliet touched her arm to indicate that it was time to return to their own desks.

They retraced their steps. As she stepped back in the office, Caroline looked at the clock on the wall. It was already twelve o'clock! The morning had flown by.

Juliet followed Caroline's gaze and nodded. "Lunchtime already!" she confirmed. "You're welcome to get something to eat at the dining room down the hall, Caroline. Or you may want to go out, which is what the other interns usually do. I'd love to have a meal with you myself, but I think I'd better stay in and work through lunch today. Some other time, though. I'll see you back here around one and we'll get you started, all right?"

With an encouraging smile, Juliet disappeared into the inner office. Caroline walked slowly to the work station she'd been assigned and tucked her briefcase under the desk. As she did so, she glanced surreptitiously at the other interns. The two boys and two of the girls were heading for the door in a laughing, cliquish group. Caroline swallowed her disappointment. It sure didn't look as if they were going to invite her along.

Well, I have plenty to do on my own, she consoled herself. *With an hour I can grab a quick bite to eat and still have some time to check out the neighborhood. There are bound to be some interesting stores nearby, maybe even a park.*

Caroline was halfway to the door when a soft voice stopped her. "Caroline, I'm on my way out, too. Would you like to have lunch together?"

She turned around. One of the interns, a pretty girl with lots of dark, wavy hair, had walked up behind her. Caroline racked her brain trying to remember the girl's name. She was fairly sure it was one of the "R"s—either Rosemary or Rachel, but for the life of her she couldn't figure out which. "That would be great." Caroline accepted the invitation with a smile, hoping she didn't sound too desperate for company. "Thanks, R—" Caroline faltered, blushing.

"Rachel Blum." The other girl giggled, her brown eyes sparkling. "Don't worry, it's impossible to remember so many names at once. There are still a few people I blank out on and I've been here since May!"

They walked together down the hall and rode the elevator to the main floor. "So, Caroline, do you live in New York?" Rachel asked, taking advantage of the privacy of the elevator to touch up her red lipstick.

"Oh, no." Caroline laughed, secretly pleased that Rachel could mistake her for a native. "I'm from San Francisco. I'm only in New York for a month with my cousin."

"Oh, so you go to college in California," Rachel presumed. "Stanford? Berkeley? UCLA?"

Caroline looked away self-consciously. "Actually, I just graduated from high school. I'll be starting at Colorado University, in Boulder, in a couple of months. What about you?"

The elevator swished to a stop, and the two girls stepped out. Rachel dug Caroline in the side with her elbow, nodding towards an extremely good-looking man in a sharp, double-breasted suit. "One of the great things about New York— loads of gorgeous men!" she whispered, making Caroline grin. "I'll be a sophomore at New York University in September, but my family lives in Boston," Rachel continued.

"How come you didn't go home for the summer?" Caroline asked.

"Oh, I was having so much fun in New York I decided to stay right through till fall semester. I feel like I know Boston inside and out—New York is still new for me. The U.N. is my first real summer job," she told Caroline. "I've always waitressed back home during vacations. The tips aren't as good at the U.N.," she joked. "Seriously, though, this is really intense in comparison."

Caroline was glad to hear that she wasn't the only person who found the U.N. intimidating. "It's my first real job, too, I guess," she confided as they left the building and strolled down the steps to the sidewalk, where they melted into the lunchtime crowd. "Are they working you very hard?"

Rachel had led the way to a small, bustling deli where they picked up bulging submarine sandwiches and icy bottles of fruit-flavored seltzer. "It's not bad at all," she promised Caroline. "The hours are pretty regular and it's fascinating exposure. The people you meet! Wait until you go to your first reception or cocktail party. It's a blast— the interns get to mingle with famous diplomats and even royalty from all these far-out countries, some of which I'd never even heard of before this summer."

Caroline was impressed. Wait till she told Chrissy about this angle of her job! She bet *Heart Throb* didn't have anything as exciting to offer in the way of fringe benefits.

It was a warm sunny day, so Caroline and Rachel took their lunches to a bench in a small park a few blocks from the U.N. They gabbed for the entire lunch hour. Rachel had a million suggestions for Caroline and Chrissy about places to walk, shop, and eat and she was also cooperative about filling Caroline in on the other interns. "Tad Lewiston is from Harvard, Paco Estiban is a few years ahead of me at NYU, and Rosemary Grissom and Claudine Platte both go to Middlebury College." Rachel tapped them off on her fingers as she spoke.

"Are they . . . friendly?" Caroline asked cautiously, between bites of her sub.

Rachel seemed to pick up on Caroline's uncertain tone. "You mean because of the way they bolted out to lunch without even saying boo to you?" she said frankly. "You know, I'm sure they would have asked you along but they probably assumed you were doing something with Juliet on your first day here. They're all pretty cool people. I'm sure you'll fit in just fine."

"Thanks." Caroline smiled back. She felt better about being new and inexperienced now that she'd already made a friend. "I really think I'm going to like this internship."

At one o'clock, Caroline and Rachel hurried back inside. This time as she entered the French interpreters' center, Caroline felt more as if she belonged there. She was still a little anxious, but at least now she knew she could turn to Rachel for help if she needed it. She settled in at her desk, slinging her blazer over the back of her chair, and feeling very professional. Juliet was about to instruct her on transcribing her first tape! Actually, Juliet had said that the first few times she'd be "proofing," or double-checking, the work of one of the other interns, but soon she'd be on her own. When she started college in the fall, she would already have the experience of working in an important position at the United Nations! As Caroline slipped her headphones on, she was happier than ever that she and Chrissy had taken the plunge and come to New York.

Chapter 5

The same morning, Chrissy stood on the sidewalk in front of the Flatiron Building, staring up at the odd-looking structure. Shaped like a piece of pie and made of dirty stone, the building was wedged in between Fifth Avenue and Broadway, where the two avenues intersected 23rd Street. Chrissy had learned from her book about New York that the Flatiron had been the first skyscraper in the city. It was practically an antique, and a lot different from the sleek, modern glass-and-steel office buildings of midtown. Uncle Richard had explained that publishing offices were often less conventional in appearance and operation than those of other more straitlaced businesses. In other words, she could expect just about anything!

Chrissy crossed the rushing stream of pedestrians and pushed open the door. Inside, the lobby was dark and cool. The antique elevator shook and rattled like a tractor-combine on its last legs and Chrissy was relieved to step off quickly at the seventh floor. She emerged at one end of a short hall. The pink door at the opposite end read simply HEART THROB in plain black letters. Chrissy felt a little disappointed as she approached it. So far, this wasn't looking like a very glamorous organization.

She changed her mind the instant she entered the *Heart Throb* office. Rock music pulsed out of invisible speakers; a jungle of potted plants practically obscured the reception desk; and one entire wall was covered by an enormous reproduction of a *Heart Throb* cover that was lit up from the back so that it glowed. Even the receptionist was out of the ordinary. She was absolutely beautiful, with waist-long black hair; she wore an Indian sari shot through with silver threads, and a red jewel on her forehead.

It was a few moments before Chrissy realized she was standing just inside the door with her mouth hanging open. She snapped it shut and strode up to the reception desk to introduce herself. But the phone rang incessantly, keeping the receptionist occupied. No sooner had she passed along one call than another one came through.

The extra minutes gave Chrissy a chance to check out the office some more—and also a chance to feel even more nervous about her new job. *What am I doing in a place like this?* she thought helplessly. *I'm an Iowa farm girl, not a chic city socialite! Well, at least I know a lot about entertainment—at least I think I do. A movie a week in San Francisco counts for something, doesn't it?* Chrissy sighed. *But I could never hope to fit in with the people here. I bet all the celebrities will think I'm a real hick.* She glanced at the picture of the glamorous model in the giant magazine cover. Although Chrissy had developed a new, more sophisticated style while she'd lived in San Francisco, she suspected she was still universes away from the kind of style she was going to encounter working at *Heart Throb*. *At least I no longer wear those gingham-print dresses like I used to wear to church in Danbury.*

The receptionist interrupted Chrissy's anxious musings, greeting her in a low, musical voice. "Hello. You must be Angela, the model for Stephen's harvest-moon fashion shoot."

"Oh, no, I'm just Chrissy Madden, the new intern," Chrissy stuttered in explanation. Then a bright smile flashed across her face. The receptionist had mistaken her for a model! Maybe she was more stylish than she'd thought.

"Oh, Chrissy, of course." The beautiful receptionist took a closer look at Chrissy and nodded as if wondering how she could have made such a mistake. She wasn't being rude, but still Chrissy's exuberance deflated somewhat. "I'm Karma. I do the phones. And since they're not ringing for a second, I'll take you around the corner to

Sophie's office. She's the only editor without an intern these days and she's dying to meet you."

Chrissy followed Karma, marveling at the way she could walk on the highly polished parquet floor without making a sound. Chrissy herself clattered like a colt in her unaccustomed heels.

The entertainment editor's office was the first in a long hall that opened out at the end into what looked to Chrissy like a garage ready for a tag sale. The door to the office was ajar, and instead of rock music, jazz strains drifted out to meet Chrissy's ears. Inside she noticed a woman who didn't look much older than herself bent over a desk littered with papers and photographs. She looked up when Chrissy entered and smiled.

"Chrissy! Not a moment too soon. Can I ever use you!" She stepped around the desk to shake Chrissy's hand. "I'm Sophie Ambrose."

"It's nice to meet you," Chrissy said sincerely. She turned to wave a thank you to Karma, who was already sprinting back to the buzzing phones. "I'm really excited about working at *Heart Throb*. I really appreciate being offered this internship."

Sophie laughed. "I should be thanking you! My assistant left a month ago and I've been running myself ragged ever since. You'll definitely be earning your keep. But you'll have a lot of fun while you're at it. I mean, this is *Heart Throb*, not *The Wall Street Journal!*"

Sophie had been perched on the edge of her desk and now she hopped to her feet. She was petite, a couple of inches shorter than Chrissy, but she radiated a forceful energy. "How about a grand tour, Chrissy? Then we can talk about ourselves and your job and all that."

Not waiting for an answer, Sophie took Chrissy by the arm and propelled her out into the hall. She didn't bother knocking on doors, but simply popped into office after office, introducing Chrissy to everyone in sight. Chrissy met editors, interns, graphic artists, and photographers. The huge, cluttered room at the end of the hall was a studio of sorts where the editors worked on the layout of the magazine's pages on large drafting tables. Opening off the studio were smaller studios where photo sessions took place. Sophie let Chrissy peek into one. Inside, a pencil-thin girl with a cloud of white-blond hair was pouting and posing while a photographer shot several pictures in rapid succession. Chrissy gaped. She recognized the beautiful, heart-shaped face as the girl on the cover of this month's *Seventeen*!

Sophie whirled Chrissy back into her own office and Chrissy collapsed somewhat inelegantly into a big red vinyl chair facing Sophie's desk. Chrissy prided herself on having as much stamina as a Kentucky Derby winner, but she had a feeling she might just have met her match. She got a strong impression that Sophie Ambrose wasn't the type to bother with coffee breaks or Sunday afternoon naps.

While Sophie talked about her job as entertainment editor of *Heart Throb* magazine, a position she'd held now for a year, Chrissy took the opportunity to study the person she'd be working with for the next month. Sophie's iron-straight auburn hair fell to her chin and swung from side to side when she talked. The cut accentuated her slender neck, and her black sleeveless dress made a striking contrast with her ivory complexion. Sophie's neck, wrists, and ears glittered with silver—Chrissy counted three pierces in each lobe. "Funky"—that was the word Caroline would use to describe Sophie.

"That's my job," Sophie concluded, tugging on one long earring. "Now for your job. For the most part, you'll assist me in editing articles—movie reviews, interviews, and so on. I write some of the movie reviews myself and after you've had a little practice editing, I'll take you along to a premiere and you can co-write a review."

Chrissy practically levitated out of her chair. A movie premiere! She pictured herself stepping from a stretch limousine, hurrying into the theater on the arm of Tom Selleck, holding a gloved hand to her face to avoid the glare of flashbulbs. She was wearing a long, clinging dress covered with sequins. As Tom Selleck put a muscular arm around her to shield her from the photographers, he smiled into her eyes with appreciation. "You look spectacular tonight, Christina," he said in a deep manly voice. His famous dimples flashed, just for her. "I wish we could have stayed at home instead of coming to another one of these boring premieres."

"Me, too," she breathed, meaningfully fluttering her impossibly long eyelashes.

Sophie kept talking, not seeming to notice Chrissy's dazzled expression. "In addition you'll help me schedule interviews and act as a contact between the writer who'll do the interview and the person being interviewed."

Chrissy couldn't refrain from interrupting. "You mean I'll talk to *celebrities*?"

Sophie smiled. "You'll probably talk to celebrities' secretaries or agents. But that's the next best thing. As for your work space, there's a desk for you in the office next door and a phone that's hooked up to my line so you can pick up my calls when I can't. You met Malcolm's intern Jackie, and Bernard, who's working with the fashion editor, right? They're in there, too. So it'll be cozy."

Chrissy nodded. She'd only gotten a glimpse of Jackie and Bernard but they both seemed friendly. She liked meeting new people and was glad she'd be sharing an office. It would have been sort of lonely on her own.

Chrissy sat forward in her chair, her eyes sparkling. "When do I get started?" she asked eagerly.

Sophie stood up and beat Chrissy to the door. "Right now."

"And that's all they let you do all day?" Chrissy wrinkled her nose dubiously. "Listen to tapes and type out what they say on a computer?"

It was evening and Chrissy and Caroline were leaning on the rail of the Staten Island ferry. After work they'd met at the loft and then taken the subway down to the Battery, the southernmost tip of Manhattan. The breeze on the water was cool and salty. Behind the ferry, now cruising back to the city, the sun dipped lower over the Hudson River, casting a rosy glow on the buildings and touching the Statue of Liberty with orange shadows.

Caroline nodded. "My brain is completely exhausted. I can't seem to get the French vocabulary out of it. It feels like I'm still wearing headphones!"

"Well, no offense but that sounds sort of boring to me," Chrissy had to admit. She adjusted her sunglasses. "I mean you might as well still be in school!"

"Boring?" Caroline repeated her cousin's word in a tone of righteous indignation. "*Boring?* Chrissy, working at the United Nations, even as a junior translator, could never be boring." She tossed a lock of windblown hair back from her face. "At least, not for someone who cares about what's going on in the world," she added.

"Maybe so," Chrissy conceded with a grin. "But I'd go crazy being plugged into a tape recorder for eight hours on end. *My* job is something new every minute. Today I ran around nonstop!"

"You ran around nonstop, but to what purpose?" Caroline asked irritably.

"To a lot of purpose!" Chrissy hotly defended

herself. "*Heart Throb* happens to be a major magazine. Top writers and photographers and all sorts of exciting people work there. I happen to have seen the model who was on the cover of *Seventeen* last month, in the flesh!"

"Big deal!" Caroline scoffed as the ferry bounced over the wake caused by a passing freighter. "I suppose some teeny-bopper model is as important as a diplomat who helps form policies on global issues!"

"Well, excuse me, Henrietta Kissinger!" Chrissy declared with a sniff. "More people would probably recognize her face than one of your fuddy-duddy old diplomats! More people are probably interested in fashion and movie stars and stuff than the boring old U.N.!"

"Humph!" Caroline turned her back on her cousin and Chrissy did likewise. They didn't speak for the rest of the ferry ride, not even as they disembarked from the ferry when it pulled up at the pier.

As they walked up the pier to the street side by side in silence, Chrissy darted a sheepish look at Caroline. "I'm sorry, Cara," she apologized. "I didn't mean what I said about the U.N. just now. I guess, well, I guess it's a lucky thing you're there instead of me!"

Caroline couldn't help giggling. "You're not kidding," she agreed. "I think we both got the kind of internship we wanted. Mine is educational—"

"And mine is fun!"

They reached the street and Chrissy checked her watch. It was seven-thirty. "Now, how about getting something to eat?" she suggested. "I can't ever seem to get used to these late dinners. At home we would have already washed the dishes."

"Well, Rachel from work told me about a really good restaurant that's only a few blocks away from the loft back in SoHo. It's called the Orange Blossom Cafe. Let's try it."

Fifteen minutes later the girls were sitting at a rickety cast-iron table on the sidewalk in front of the cafe, drinks on the table before them.

Chrissy took a long sip from the tall glass of mango juice she'd ordered as an experiment. She made a wry face. "Wanna trade?" she asked hopefully.

Caroline laughed and slid her diet soda across the table. "Help yourself, Chrissy. I'm sorry I made fun of *Heart Throb* before, too. It does sound pretty neat. I can't believe you get to go to an actual movie premiere!"

"*We're* going to go," Chrissy corrected Caroline. "You know, nobody attends those functions without an escort!"

They were still giggling when the waiter arrived with a basket full of bread sticks. The second his back was turned, they dug in voraciously. "Any cute guys at *Heart Throb*?" Caroline asked.

Chrissy munched on a bread stick thoughtfully. "Bernard's distinguished-looking and really nice. He wears very funky clothes and he's a laugh a minute. But I can't say I experienced love at first sight. There's another intern, José, who's pretty cute. He's from Madrid. He's kind of the dark and mysterious type."

Caroline raised an eyebrow, interested. "Sounds good to me!"

Chrissy shrugged. "He just *looks* mysterious. When you talk to him, he's as normal as the next guy! I don't know. I guess neither of them is my type."

Caroline sighed. "I don't know if there's much prospect for romance at the U.N., either," she admitted, stirring the mango juice with a straw. "I told you about the other interns besides Rachel. Tad and Rosemary, and Paco and Claudine make a pretty tight foursome. But this was just our first day," she added optimistically. "It's a little too soon to throw in the towel!"

"That reminds me!" Caroline practically fell off her chair at Chrissy's shriek. "Guess where we're going on Wednesday night?"

Caroline shook her head, mystified. "I can't guess." She wrinkled her nose. "I'm afraid to guess!"

Chrissy paused dramatically, drawing out her moment of suspense. "The Palladium," she announced in a deep, meaningful voice. "It's just about the hottest club in town, and we have tickets to a private party there!"

"A private party!" Caroline was as impressed as Chrissy had hoped.

The girls were now digging into exotic tossed

salads garnished with kiwi fruit and cashews. "Janel, the night-life editor, gave me the tickets," Chrissy explained as she speared a carrot slice. "All the interns got a pair. And this is the best part." Chrissy leaned forward in her wobbly cast-iron chair. "It's a party for . . ."

Caroline shook her head in disbelief when Chrissy mentioned the name of a rising young pop-music star whose latest single had gone to the top of the charts. She forgot that half an hour earlier she had snobbily made fun of Chrissy's fascination with teeny-bopper celebrities. "Pinch me. I think I'm dreaming," Caroline said.

"It's absolutely true." Chrissy polished off her salad with satisfaction. "A private party at the Palladium. Wouldn't you say that's starting things off in style?"

Chapter 6

"I can't go to the Palladium," Chrissy wailed. "I don't have anything to wear!"

Caroline couldn't help laughing. "What do you mean, you don't have anything to wear? Aren't you the girl who arrived in New York City last weekend with a suitcase the size of a small car?"

Chrissy stood in her underwear surveying all the clothes hanging in the large walk-in closet. "I don't have anything *right* to wear," she said sadly. "The Palladium's the most chic club in the city. Take a look at my clothes. Do they say 'chic' to you?"

They didn't, but Caroline didn't want to discourage her cousin. They were running late as it was. "Chrissy, I remember when you didn't care what you wore and you always managed to look fantastic anyway."

"Well, I care now." Chrissy sounded earnest. "My new friends from *Heart Throb* are going to be there, and hundreds of celebrities. I don't want to look like Judy Garland in *The Wizard of Oz*. Everyone will know I'm from Iowa! I'll be a laughingstock."

Caroline had ducked into the bathroom to reposition the rhinestone-studded barrette that was holding back her silky hair. "Chrissy, think about what happened the last couple of times you pretended to be someone you're not," she shouted in the direction of the closet. "If anything, the hundreds of celebrities at the Palladium will be intrigued by someone from Iowa! You're sure to be the only one."

Chrissy laughed. Caroline was right, as usual. She'd often felt insecure when she lived with the Kirbys in San Francisco, especially in the beginning. Caroline and all her friends were so cool and grown-up, so different from her own friends back home in Danbury.

"Hey, Cara, remember Hunter Bryce?" Chrissy shouted back with a grin.

"Do I ever!" Caroline replied. "I don't know why you thought you had to pretend you were a cultured world traveler to impress him. He didn't seem to mind when he found out you were from Iowa."

Chrissy pulled out an electric-blue jumpsuit that was usually her trusty standby, then quickly put it back in the closet. It just wasn't right for tonight. "Yeah, I went to all those horrible concerts and films that I couldn't understand. I even ate raw fish at that sushi bar! And all for nothing. Hunter turned out to be a real jerk." She paused. "Cara, you're right. It's a lot safer just to be me—more fun, too."

"I'm glad that's settled!" Caroline called.

Chrissy glanced again at the clothes in her closet. "But I still don't know what to wear! *Help!*"

Caroline rejoined Chrissy in the closet and placed her hands on her hips, ready to get down to business. "Well, first of all, Chrissy, chic doesn't necessarily mean fancy. I personally think the simple look is the most effective." Caroline herself was dressed in a short, black body-hugging dress, her only accessories a rhinestone necklace and matching earrings. She scanned Chrissy's wardrobe with a practiced eye. "Here. Try this."

Thirty seconds later Caroline had a loose long-sleeved T-shirt, a denim miniskirt, and a black leather belt studded with turquoise and silver laid out on the bed.

Chrissy stared at the clothes and then started to smile. In five minutes she was dressed, having added a pair of low-heeled cowboy boots and chunky turquoise earrings to the ensemble. Caroline couldn't help being pleased with her handiwork. The outfit suited Chrissy's breezy, natural style and flattered her curvy figure. All of a sudden Caroline felt plain in comparison. But there wasn't time for her to have a clothing crisis, too.

"Ready to go?" Chrissy asked, her voice high-pitched with excitement.

"You bet!"

The loft was on a fairly quiet street, so it was a few minutes before the two girls were able to hail a taxi. Once inside, Chrissy gave the driver the address of the Palladium. He pulled away from the curb with a squeal of tires and Chrissy was flung back against the seat.

"Oof!" she squeaked, the breath nearly knocked out of her. She giggled and lowered her voice so only Caroline could hear her. "Did I say 'Step on it'?"

Caroline grinned. "You don't need to say 'Step on it' to a New York cabbie," she whispered back. "They burn rubber as a matter of course."

The driver had flipped on the radio and the taxi was resounding with very loud music sung in a foreign language the girls couldn't identify. Caroline looked more than a little nervous as they swerved out into traffic on a crowded avenue. Chrissy laughed at her cousin's expression. "This is fun!" she declared, rolling down her window to get the full effect of the city speeding past. Her hair whipped every which way in the rushing wind. "Kind of like riding a runaway horse in a tornado!"

Caroline squeezed her eyes shut as they missed another speeding taxi by inches. "Don't tell me," she said weakly. "Just let me know when we get there. I'm not going to look."

But when Chrissy yelled at the top of her lungs a moment later, Caroline's eyes did pop open. To her horror, Chrissy was hanging halfway out the taxi's open window.

"Stop the car!" Caroline screeched to the oblivious driver.

Scowling, the driver pulled over with another squeal of the tires. Meanwhile, Caroline had grabbed Chrissy by the belt and yanked her back inside the cab. Thinking they wanted to be dropped off, the driver turned around to request his fare.

But Caroline was more concerned about her cousin. "Are you absolutely insane, Chrissy? Where did you think you were going?"

"My purse flew out the window!" Chrissy cried, her blue eyes clouded with distress.

"And you were just going to fly out after it?" Caroline snapped, shaking her head in disbelief.

"Well . . ." Chrissy shrugged.

"You scared me half to death!"

"Oh, I'm sorry, Cara! But I lost my purse! We have to find it."

The taxi driver demanded his fare again, this time impatiently.

"Could you wait one minute?" Caroline asked politely. "We lost something but we should be able to find it quickly. You could leave the meter running and—"

"Unh-uh." The cabbie shook his head firmly.

"No waiting. It's a busy night, you know?"

"Oh, okay." Caroline unzipped her own small shoulder bag and paid the fare. The driver took it, then sped off without another word, leaving the two cousins standing on the sidewalk. Slowly, they retraced their route until they reached the point where Chrissy thought she'd accidentally let go of the purse. Caroline raised her eyebrows. "Chrissy, we'll never find it," she predicted, placing her hands on her hips in frustration.

Chrissy looked around. Cars and taxis dashed down the one-way avenue four abreast and the traffic was continuous. Streetlights and headlights lit up the evening sky, but still it was too dark to be able to distinguish her small black clutch among all the other unidentifiable objects in the street. She had to admit that Caroline was right.

Chrissy stamped her foot. "Well, there goes our night!" she announced, sitting down on the curb dejectedly.

"What was in the purse?" Caroline asked, opting not to take a seat herself on the dirty concrete.

"Just a few dollars and my Iowa driver's license. *And*," Chrissy added, with mournful emphasis, "the tickets to the party at the Palladium."

Caroline tapped her toe on the sidewalk, considering the situation. "It's not the end of the world, Chrissy," she said reasonably. "And you know, Rachel was telling me today about the way these clubs work. A lot of times they have supposedly private parties but they give out invitations by the handful. Maybe when we get there we'll see somebody you know from *Heart Throb* and they could take us as their guests. Or maybe we'll get in on our own—we'd just have to pay at the door. I probably have enough money."

Chrissy sprang to her feet, injected with new life. "That would be fantastic. We've got to give it a try!"

The cousins checked the street signs and discovered that they were only a few blocks from the Palladium, so instead of taking another taxi they walked the rest of the way. As they approached the popular nightclub they could see a crowd of people on the sidewalk out front, pressing against the entrance. They joined the crowd at the fringes, and Chrissy examined the sea of faces, hoping to spot someone from work, but with no luck.

Caroline turned to a girl standing near them. "What's going on?" she asked, trying to sound casual and not like someone who was going to a New York nightclub for the first time.

The girl shrugged. "It's a big party and it's already packed. They're not letting in very many people off the street, unless you have tickets, that is."

Caroline peered toward the door. Three burly bouncers in Palladium T-shirts were effectively blocking the entrance. One of them, however, was scanning the waiting crowd. Every now and then he'd point to somebody, and that person would be admitted.

"I don't know, Chrissy," she whispered, crossing her arms. The night breeze was cool on her bare skin. "It looks like they're picking a few random people out of the crowd to go in, but I have a feeling—"

Just then, the bouncer gestured to Chrissy. "Me?" Chrissy yelped. She did a little excited hop on the sidewalk. She started forward and then remembered Caroline. "Oh, Cara . . ." Her voice trailed off doubtfully. "I'll wait for you. They'll probably get to you in a minute."

Caroline's face had gone pink with mortification. They'd picked Chrissy out of the crowd and not her? Chrissy, who wouldn't even have known what to wear if Caroline hadn't dressed her?

"Go ahead, Chrissy," Caroline said, clenching her teeth in an effort to sound controlled and nonchalant. "If you don't take this chance, you probably won't get another one."

When Chrissy didn't budge, Caroline gave her a slight shove forward. "I'll see you later," she said in a tight voice.

Chrissy looked from Caroline's stiff face toward the entrance of the Palladium and then back again. "I don't want to go in without you," she said. "Come on."

She took Caroline's hand and pulled her through the crowd toward the entrance. But when they got there, the bouncer looked at them without sympathy.

"Ladies, where do you think you're going?"

"Inside," Chrissy replied. "I thought you said we could go in."

The bouncer shook his head and smirked. "No. I said *you* could go in. Your friend, she stays out here and waits her turn."

Caroline's face flushed even pinker, and she felt as if everyone in the huge crowd on the sidewalk was staring at her. She couldn't even disappear into the crowd because Chrissy was still clutching her hand.

"I know! I'm going to talk to the manager, that's what I'll do," Chrissy decided cheerfully. "I'll be right back, Cara. I'll get this all straightened out."

Caroline's jaw dropped. After all this, Chrissy was still going in without her, on the flimsy excuse of trying to talk to the manager! "You do that, Chrissy," Caroline said, practically choking on her words.

"I'll be right back," Chrissy repeated in a firm voice. "Oh, Cara?" Chrissy turned and looked back at her cousin appealingly. "Can I borrow a couple of bucks? In case I have to pay for a ticket for you . . ."

Caroline whipped open her pocketbook and pulled a ten-dollar bill from her wallet. She practically threw it at Chrissy. "Thanks!" Chrissy called over her shoulder as she marched purposefully through the doorway.

Caroline wished she could sink right into the sidewalk. She was pretty sure she'd never been so humiliated. For a moment, she hesitated.

There *was* a small chance Chrissy would be able to talk the manager into letting her into the club, too. But all of a sudden, Caroline didn't want to wait around to find out. A public scene with the Palladium manager would make her look ten times more idiotic than she did right now.

"This is turning out to be a great night," she muttered to herself as she turned on her heel and squeezed her way back through the crowd and stalked away from the Palladium. She knew she shouldn't resent Chrissy for what had just happened. Chrissy hadn't meant to lose the tickets; she couldn't help it if she looked so cute with her corn-yellow hair and funky cowgirl outfit. And she knew Chrissy honestly was trying to talk to the manager. But still . . . *Grrr*, Cara grumbled silently.

At the corner, Caroline held her hand in the air, praying for a taxi to stop quickly. Her anger hadn't warmed her up; she was still chilled. But as if to make her feel even more rejected, about twenty cabs sailed by her before one finally stopped. Caroline climbed in and gave the address of the loft in a forlorn tone.

Sometimes cab drivers were friendly and chatty, but this one seemed to be feeling as glum as she was. He had the radio tuned to a classical station and the mournful wail of violins in a minor key brought tears of self-pity to Caroline's light-blue eyes. She looked out the window, sniffling discreetly.

Once she was home at the apartment, her

annoyance faded and Caroline just felt lonely.
*Here I am, in this enormous city where a million
things are going on twenty-four hours a day, and
I'm by myself, with nobody to talk to,* she thought,
dropping onto one of the living-room couches
and kicking off her shoes. If she were in San
Francisco, she'd have her parents to talk with, or
she could call Tracy or Maria or Justine. . . .

"Or Luke," Caroline said out loud, addressing
one of the statues. Luke's name seemed to echo
off the walls, or maybe it was just echoing inside
her head. Caroline sighed a deep, shaky sigh. No
matter what she'd said to Luke when they broke
up about not needing him, right now she felt as if
she would give anything to be with him, to hold
him close and pour out all her feelings to him.
Luke had always understood her in a way no one
else ever had.

"What's stopping me?" Caroline asked the
statue.

The statue didn't answer and so Caroline
responded to her own question. "Nothing's stopping me. And it's an hour, or is it two hours
earlier in Iowa. They'll still be up. . . ."

There was an ultramod telephone on top of the
solid black marble block that served as a coffee
table. Caroline stared at it for a full minute, and
then, her heart pounding irregularly, she put out
her hand to pick up the receiver. When she
touched the cool plastic, however, her determi-
nation deserted her. She couldn't call Luke in a
moment of weakness. He hadn't called her once

since they'd broken up—and he'd certainly made it clear he didn't need *her*. Besides, he was probably out on a date with his new farm-girl steady!

Caroline turned away from the phone. She tried to feel disgusted with Luke, but she still just felt lonely. She closed her eyes, tired. All of a sudden she was with Luke and they were walking hand in hand together through a field bright with grass and flowers. Caroline could almost feel the warm pressure of Luke's fingers and smell the fresh scent of a Danbury spring. *I'd rather be there than here*, she thought sadly. New York City wasn't all *that* exciting. It was grimy and loud and alienating. There were so many people but none of them were connected with each other. She might as well be the only person on the entire island of Manhattan tonight.

A fat tear welled out of Caroline's right eye and slid silently down her cheek. She took a deep breath, ready to let out a heartfelt sob when she heard the creaking of the elevator rising. Caroline went cold right down to her bare toes as she turned on the couch to face the elevator door. Everyone knew that New York was the crime capital of the United States. And now she was about to experience it first hand!

Calm down, Cara, she told herself. *It's probably nothing. But only people with a key to the loft apartment can use the elevator!* a small voice reminded her as the creaking came nearer.

Caroline looked around her rapidly. There was no place to hide—or was there? Jumping to her feet, she made a dash for the largest of the surrealist sculptures—a wide, amoeba-shaped blob. She ducked behind it, cowering down so the top of her head wouldn't show. *Please don't see me,* she prayed desperately. *Please see the weird statues and be scared and go back down. Just leave me alone.* Caroline squeezed her eyes tightly shut and waited for her doom.

Her heart just about stopped beating as the elevator jolted to a clattering stop and the door slid slowly open. There was a footstep and then another. It sounded like a heavy man, someone wearing boots. Suddenly the intruder screamed.

Caroline's nerves were so taut that at the sound she screeched, too. She burst out from behind the sculpture to see Chrissy backed against the wall as far as she could go without going through, gaping as if she'd seen a ghost.

Relief swamped over Caroline, causing her ankles to buckle. "Chrissy!" she yelped. "You scared me half to death! I thought one of the FBI's ten most wanted was on his way up here in the elevator!"

"I could say the same for you!" Chrissy exclaimed with a giggle. "I walked in and the living room looked empty. And then I saw someone's foot sticking out from behind that sculpture!"

Caroline was so happy to see Chrissy that she forgot to be mad. "What are you doing back so early anyway?" she asked, sinking weakly onto the nearest sofa.

Chrissy stepped out of her boots by the elevator and then padded across the floor barefoot to join Caroline. "Well, I did try to talk to the manager, but the place is so big I practically got lost trying to find him," Chrissy explained. "I couldn't find any of the other kids from *Heart Throb* to help me out, either. I didn't even get to see the guest of honor! Apparently he'd left with his band after only one set." She sighed. "Oh, but Cara, I wish you could've come inside with me—the Palladium is really something to see. A couple of guys even asked me to dance, but they were pretty creepy. City slickers, you know, handing out lines like 'You must be an actress' and 'Didn't I meet you last Friday at the Limelight?'"

Caroline laughed. "Real Prince Charmings, huh?"

"You better believe it!" Chrissy declared as she tucked her feet up under her and settled back on the couch. Then she burst into a peal of giggles. "Cara, you should have seen your face when you launched out from behind that statue! Did you really think I was a ruthless killer?"

Caroline giggled at the thought of how ridiculous she must have looked. "I really thought my number was up. You should have seen your own face, Chrissy Madden! And you claim you're not scared of anything!"

"Holy mazoly. It could only happen to us," Chrissy said, laughing so hard her stomach hurt. She hiccuped her way over to the TV and flipped it on. On the screen, a green disembodied hand wiggled its way out of a swamp. Caroline squeaked.

"*Tales from the Dark Side!*" Chrissy hooted. "Wouldn't you know?"

The cousins watched television until two-thirty, devouring two batches of microwave popcorn. Finally they crawled off to bed, their eyelids drooping with fatigue.

"G'night, Cara. See you in the morning," Chrissy mumbled before she dropped off to sleep.

"Sweet dreams, Chrissy," Caroline answered softly. It was a few minutes before she dozed off herself. As she lay listening to the tree branches tapping lightly on the window next to her bed, the image of Luke popped back into her head. She might be in a new city meeting new people and doing new things, but she hadn't forgotten him yet, and something told Caroline she wasn't going to, ever.

Chapter 7

"Rachel, you've lived in the city for a year," Chrissy said, looking up from a bubbling saucepan, wooden spoon in hand. "You could give us some tips on how to score points with New York boys!"

Caroline had invited Rachel Blum, her new friend from the U.N., over for dinner, and the three girls were busy in the kitchen. Rachel was in charge of the salad and Caroline was making Alfredo sauce for the pasta while Chrissy kept an eye on the tortellini.

Rachel giggled. "Chrissy, a guy is a guy, whether he lives in New York or Alaska. I have a feeling," she added as she sliced a carrot, "that you and Caroline aren't going to have much of a problem meeting people at the Limelight tonight."

At work that day Chrissy had received passes to another "private party," this time at the Limelight, an old church that had been remodeled into a popular dance club. Caroline had agreed to give the club scene another try, but she wasn't taking any chances. She planned to carry the tickets herself, and no matter how nice a night it was, the windows were going to stay closed during the cab ride.

"But the guys at the Palladium the other night looked so . . ." Chrissy searched for the right word and then settled on one of her cousin's favorite adjectives. ". . . so sophisticated. I mean, they don't dress like the boys at home in Iowa or even the ones in San Francisco. They all look like they stepped right out of *G.Q.* magazine."

"Seriously, don't sweat it." Rachel vigorously shook a bottle of Italian dressing. "It always seems like the more duded out a guy is, the more of a jerk he is. Or else he looks fantastic but he's totally shy and couldn't get his mouth open to ask you to dance for his life."

"Speaking of duded out," Caroline interjected, her voice teasing. She paused in the act of grating a chunk of fresh Parmesan cheese. "You should probably start getting ready now, Chrissy. Last time it took you a whole hour just to figure out what you *weren't* going to wear!"

Chrissy tipped her chin up and gave Caroline a superior look. "For your information, Miss

Smarty Pants, I already have my outfit planned! I bought a new dress during my lunch hour."

"A new dress? Well, excuse me!" Caroline winked at Rachel and went on grating the cheese.

Chrissy gave the tortellini an impatient stir. "Well, aren't you going to ask me what the dress looks like?"

"Okay." Caroline relented. "We're dying to hear about it. Tell us."

"All right." Chrissy grinned. "Since you asked!" She dropped the spoon against the side of the pot and ran into the bedroom. She was back in a flash, gingerly carrying the hanger in one hand and holding the dress up against her body. The dress was a deep cherry-red color with a short skirt and beads sewn around the neckline and the edges of the sleeves. "Isn't it cute! I know I'm supposed to be on a budget when I'm in New York but I couldn't resist. And anyhow, it was on sale."

Chrissy stood there happily as Caroline and Rachel admired her new dress. She had tried it on just for fun, but the second it was zipped and she got a look at herself in the mirror, she was sold. It made her feel so chic, so New York. Wearing it, she'd be able to walk into a club like the Limelight feeling as if she owned the place. *This is the life*! she thought, carefully replacing the dress in the closet.

"Are you sure you don't want to go with us?" Caroline was saying to Rachel as she set three places on the far side of the kitchen counter above the row of high stools.

"Thanks a mil," Rachel said, popping a cherry tomato in her mouth, "but for some reason I'm really tired tonight. It's about all I can do to stand up—I'd never manage dancing! But definitely count me in next time you go out."

Quickly, Chrissy resumed her post at the stove—just in time, as the water was about to boil over. "The tortellini's ready," she announced. "Let's eat!"

Caroline raised her glass of milk. "Maybe we should have a toast," she suggested, looking to Chrissy and Rachel for inspiration.

"Let's see." Chrissy's eyes twinkled. "Here's to meeting Mr. Perfect at the Limelight!"

Rachel glanced from Chrissy to Caroline. "I think you'd better make that Mr. Perfect and his best friend," she corrected.

Caroline laughed. "I'll drink to that!"

The Limelight was already packed when the cousins arrived at ten o'clock, although it was still early by New York City standards. Caroline held her breath as she and Chrissy squeezed through the crush inside the entrance, heading for one of the sitting nooks where it looked like there might be more room. "This is amazing," Caroline whispered, coughing as a passing girl puffed cigarette smoke in her face. "I guess if we want to meet people, we're in the right place. Half the city must be here!"

Chrissy nodded. "And let me tell you, this is nothing compared to the mob at the Palladium last week," she said, adopting the voice of experience. "But there'll be space on the dance floor and that's what matters!" She glanced around, her bright eyes inspecting the men in the room.

"Hey, Cara, he's kind of cute," she observed in a loud whisper.

Caroline jumped as she felt Chrissy's elbow dig into her side. She followed the direction of Chrissy's eyes. "Where? Oh, him? He's not bad," Caroline conceded. Then to her surprise, she found herself jolted to her feet. Chrissy had grabbed her hand and was hauling her through the clusters of people in the direction of the good-looking guy.

Caroline put on the brakes, doing her best to dig her heels into the linoleum. Chrissy might have the nerve to charge right up to a handsome stranger and start up a conversation, but Caroline definitely did not. "Count me out, Chrissy," she said under her breath.

"Oh, c'mon, Cara, don't be shy," Chrissy urged, dragging Caroline forward despite all her efforts at retreat. "If we wanted to sit around talking to ourselves we could have stayed home. Be adventuresome for a change!"

Caroline sighed and smiled in spite of herself. Chrissy had a good point. And besides, it looked as if the boy she was after had disappeared. Chrissy hadn't lost sight of him, though, and a moment later the two girls were standing at the bar, just a yard away from him. Caroline ducked her head to hide behind her hair and busied herself ordering a club soda with lime, discreetly watching as Chrissy leaned casually against the bar and smiled her friendliest, most irresistible smile.

"Hi, there. Do you come here often?" Caroline's hand froze as she was reaching for her drink. *Chrissy did not just say that,* she told herself firmly. *Even she couldn't be that gauche!*

Caroline peeked through her hair in time to see the boy raise his eyebrows at Chrissy and then turn away, shaking his head haughtily. Chrissy stood for a moment, stunned. Then she faced Caroline, her expression somewhat deflated. "What did I do wrong?" she wondered aloud.

"You've got to be kidding!" Caroline said with a laugh. "Chrissy, you're the one who was telling me just the other night how much you hated it when guys use tacky lines on you. You just threw that guy the oldest, most unoriginal line in the book!"

Chrissy thought back and then she burst out laughing. "Holy mazoly, I did, didn't I? I didn't even mean it that way—I really *was* just curious to know if he'd been here before or if he was a first-timer like us!"

"Well, next time maybe you should think before you open your mouth," Caroline suggested kindly.

Next time came sooner than either of them expected. Just as Caroline was about to take the first sip of her club soda, two boys strolled up to them at the bar. They looked about the same age as the cousins, or maybe a little older, and right away Caroline found one of them distinctly attractive. He was tall and on the thin side, dressed casually but sharply in wrinkled seersucker trousers, a white Oxford shirt and a narrow navy-blue tie. His sandy brown hair flopped a little over his forehead and even in the dim light she could see a sprinkle of freckles across his straight, aristocratic nose.

All at once Caroline felt bold. She was at a sophisticated New York City nightclub presented with an opportunity to strike up a conversation with a good-looking guy. It was just too bad Luke wasn't there, too, so she could rub it right in his face.

Caroline didn't wait for Chrissy to speak first, the way she would ordinarily. She was afraid that Chrissy might blow it by saying something like "Do you come here often?" again.

"Um, hi," Caroline ventured vaguely in the direction of the two boys. Her soft voice was completely drowned out by the loud dance music.

The sandy-haired boy leaned toward her, his sleeve brushing against her. A chill ran up Caroline's bare arm. "Pardon me?" he asked.

"Hi," Caroline repeated, somewhat more forcefully. *Do I sound like an idiot or what?* she thought, wishing she'd let Chrissy do the talking after all.

If the boy thought she was an idiot, however, he did a good job of hiding it. His broad smile was warm and sincere. "Hi," he said, addressing both Caroline and Chrissy. "I'm Travis Merrill." He nodded his head at his buddy. "This is Kirk Higgins. Can we buy you girls a drink?"

"Oh, no, I already—"

Chrissy cut Caroline off before she could finish her sentence. "Sure, that would be great!" Chrissy accepted the invitation enthusiastically, meanwhile reaching nonchalantly over to the bar to shove Caroline's drink out of sight. "I'm Chrissy Madden, by the way, and this is Caroline Kirby."

The other boy, Kirk, looked from Chrissy to Caroline and back again. "Let me guess. Sisters?"

"Nope, but you're close. Cousins," Chrissy corrected him. "What about you guys?"

Kirk ran a hand through his dark hair and laughed. "Just roommates," he said, winking at Chrissy. "No permanent relation, luckily!"

"Listen to that guy. Always making jokes!" Travis waved a hand at Kirk. He turned back to Caroline. "So, what'll you have?" he asked politely.

Shyly, Caroline ordered another club soda while Chrissy decided on a grapefruit juice on the rocks. The four settled onto bar stools with their drinks. Caroline was surprised at how easy it was to carry on a lighthearted conversation with them. Travis and Kirk were both "city boys," born and raised in the New York area and currently students at Columbia University on the Upper West Side, but they weren't snobs at all. If anything, they were more impressed with Chrissy's and Caroline's exotic West Coast background.

"So it's true what those ol' Beach Boys say about California girls," Kirk observed, eyeing Chrissy admiringly.

Travis rolled his eyes for Caroline's benefit. "You'll have to excuse Mr. Suave," he said to her. "He's really got a way with words."

"Hey, I heard that." Kirk gave Travis a good-natured swat on the shoulder. "Just because you're not so gifted! He's my straight man," Kirk explained to Chrissy.

"Every clown's gotta have one!" Travis retorted with a grin.

Kirk pretended to ignore him. "Anyway, Chrissy, where were we? Oh yeah, you were telling us what it's like to be a California girl."

Chrissy laughed. "Well, other than the fact that I'm from Iowa, it's a blast!" The words came out so easily Chrissy barely realized that she'd told them she was from Iowa. There didn't seem a need to pretend to be anything but natural with Kirk and Travis.

"Do you guys surf and all that?" Travis asked Caroline.

Caroline raised her eyebrows. "Are you kidding? Do I look like a surfer?"

"Well, I don't know." Travis defended himself. "The Beach Boys have a song about a little surfer girl. . . . Oh, no, the Beach Boys again! I'm on the same wave length as Kirk. What a scary thought!"

"We're definitely not surfer girls," Chrissy confirmed. "I'd never even seen an ocean until two years ago and my first day at the beach I got knocked down by a wave and almost drowned. Nope, I don't trust water unless it's *still*. Like in a bathtub!"

Kirk guffawed and Travis smiled. Seeing that Caroline's glass was empty, Travis said, "How 'bout another round?"

Caroline didn't have a chance to answer. Chrissy had slipped down from her stool and was treating the boys to her most appealing expression. "Let's dance first," she suggested."Really work up a thirst!"

Kirk was all for it. He whirled Chrissy off in the direction of the dance floor, leaving Travis and Caroline to follow at a somewhat slower pace.

"I hope you don't mind getting stuck with me as a partner," Travis said to Caroline, his voice just a little bit uncertain. "Kirk's a lot better dancer!"

"Oh, no," Caroline said quickly. She was very happy with the way they'd paired off. "Anyhow, Chrissy's a better dancer than *me*." *Well, better at these fast free-for-all dances anyway*, she amended silently, thinking of all her years of ballet training.

"We should suit each other just fine," Travis replied, putting a hand on her back to steer her gently through the crowd to an open space on the dance floor.

Madonna's latest was reverberating around the high-ceilinged room and the strobe lights flickered in time to the beat. Travis held Caroline's eyes as they danced, and she smiled at him. Even though they weren't touching now, she could still feel his hand on her back and the electricity it had sent coursing through her. Caroline was relaxed, completely enjoying the music and enjoying Travis. They danced three straight songs, and she could tell he was having as good a time as she was.

As the fourth song faded in, Chrissy and Kirk suddenly reappeared and Kirk tapped on Travis's shoulder. "Can I cut in, sir?" Kirk intoned in a mock serious manner.

"Sure, take her," Travis joked. But he softened his offhand words by squeezing Caroline's hand warmly before he joined Chrissy, and after only two dances he suggested switching back.

Pretty soon even Chrissy was breathless, and the four retreated to the bar for another round of club sodas and grapefruit juices. Caroline was exhilarated. Dancing—and Travis's company—had gotten her adrenaline flowing. She hadn't had this much fun all summer. And the night was still young!

Then, as she squeezed the lime into her club soda, Caroline saw Travis glance at his watch and then catch Kirk's eye. *Here it comes*, she thought, surprised at how sharply disappointed she felt.

They've spent enough time with us and they're going to make up some excuse to move on.

Instead, Travis put a hand on Caroline's arm. "Hey, Caroline, Chrissy," he said. "How would you like to come back with me and Kirk to our dorm for a while? There are pretty many kids still around, taking summer classes like us, and there's a party tonight. Maybe we could check it out and order a pizza or something. After all that dancing, I'm starved!"

Chrissy looked to her cousin for confirmation before answering. Caroline was easy to read; her pleasure was written all over her face. "Sounds like fun!" Chrissy declared, tossing down her grapefruit juice in one gulp. "I'm ready when you are!"

Outside the Limelight, the night air was refreshing after the heat of close-pressed bodies inside. Travis stepped to the curb and hailed a taxi with a practiced air. Soon they were racing uptown.

Chrissy was sitting between Caroline and Kirk in the backseat of the cab. When Kirk turned to look out the window, she gave Caroline's leg a quick pinch. "Isn't this fun?" she mouthed.

Caroline nodded. It really was. Meeting Kirk and Travis—especially Travis—and being invited back to their dorm for a college party definitely qualified as the kind of real-life experience she and Chrissy were looking for in New York.

After a few minutes, the cab driver pulled up in front of a tall, building-block-style tower. Travis and Kirk split the fare and then ushered Chrissy and Caroline up the stairs and into the dormitory lobby.

"I wish it was daylight—then we could take you on a tour of campus, since you've never seen it," Travis said as they piled into the elevator. Kirk pushed the button for the eighth floor. "But it's not too safe at night."

"Maybe some other time," Chrissy suggested.

"Yeah, maybe some other time," Travis agreed, looking at Caroline.

They heard the music before the elevator door opened—Bruce Springsteen at full blast. The eighth floor hall was almost as crowded as the Limelight had been. Students in jeans and T-shirts were lounging around, drinking beer and soda out of jumbo-sized plastic cups. Kirk high-fived a dozen people as they made their way down the hall.

Most of the doors on the hall were open, and as the boys led the way to their own room, Chrissy and Caroline peeked into the other rooms they passed. Some were clean, with beds neatly made, typewriters in place on uncluttered desks and posters carefully centered on the walls. Others were chaotic, with laundry piled on the floor, record albums and books scattered everywhere, and pyramids of empty cans on the window sills.

"It's so . . . *collegiate*," Chrissy hissed under her breath to Caroline. "I can't wait until we're living in *our* dorm room!"

Caroline pictured their room at Colorado

University. Her half of it would be very neat, but Chrissy's half—that was bound to be a certified disaster area. She smiled. *I can't wait either*, she thought to herself, meaning it.

Travis and Kirk's room was a happy medium. There were about twenty pairs of shoes and sneakers on the floor, but the beds were made, and the hanging plants actually looked as if they'd been watered fairly recently. Travis gallantly offered Caroline and Chrissy the two desk chairs, and then headed back to the hall to get some sodas. Kirk, meanwhile, was already dialing the number of their favorite pizza delivery joint.

Travis returned juggling four cups filled to the brim and they settled down to wait for the pizza. They all had so much to talk about that the time passed quickly. Travis and Kirk were full of stories about college life—the parties, the classes, the dorm life—and Chrissy and Caroline drank it all in.

"Do you guys stay up partying every single night?" Chrissy asked with wide eyes. "It must be so much fun, not having any parents around to tell you to go to bed!"

"Not every night," Kirk said with a lazy smile. "More like every other night. This party out here"—he waved in the direction of the hallway—"is just heating up. It'll be going strong until four, five in the morning."

Travis was lying back on one of the beds with his hands behind his head. "Not everybody parties every other night," he said dryly. "Some people study now and then for a change."

"Don't listen to him," Kirk advised Chrissy. "College is a four-year vacation. Promise ya."

Travis's eyes met Caroline's and he smiled again in the same way he had on the dance floor. The smile gave Caroline a warm, conspiratorial feeling. While Kirk went on joking for Chrissy's entertainment, she and Travis seemed to be on the same wavelength, with a private joke all their own.

The pizza came and there was a lull in the conversation as all four dug in eagerly, even Caroline, who usually avoided fattening late-night snacks. By two in the morning, the party in the hall was in full swing. Kirk had disappeared fifteen minutes earlier after being recruited by a few of his other buddies to help play a practical joke on some girls down the hall, and Chrissy was yawning.

"I really should be getting home," she said, with an apologetic look at Caroline. "I have to get up for work pretty early tomorrow."

"But tomorrow's Saturday!" Travis protested. "C'mon, don't wimp out."

"I know," Chrissy sighed wistfully. "But I'm helping the magazine with a project. We're going to interview a new band. It should be a blast."

"We really should go," Caroline put in. It *was* late, and even though she was having fun talking to Travis, this probably was a good time to make

an exit. After all, it was a long way back to the
loft.

Travis seemed to read her mind. "Steve next
door has a car I borrow all the time," he told the
girls. "I'll run and get his keys and then I'll drive
you home."

"No, really, it's okay. We can catch a cab,"
Caroline said without much conviction. She was
too pleased and relieved at his offer to turn it
down flat.

"I want to," Travis said firmly. "Just stay put. I'll
be right back."

Chrissy and Caroline were left momentarily
alone and they took advantage of the opportunity to trade notes. "So, what do you think of
them?" Chrissy asked in her typically blunt fashion.

"They're nice," Caroline observed, more cau-
tious.

"Don't tell me they're nice," Chrissy teased.
"I've been watching you and Travis. Admit it,
there've been a few sparks!"

"What about you and Kirk?" Caroline asked.

Chrissy shrugged. "He's okay, but nothing special. I think you've really got something there
with Travis."

"I don't know," Caroline protested, blushing.
"It's not romantic at all. He's . . . *nice*. That's it."

"Sure, that's it—for now," Chrissy said in a
knowing tone.

Caroline just shook her head. *That's it*, she
repeated to herself silently. *Isn't it?*

Kirk opted to stick around at the party although he popped his head back in the door to say good-bye, and to give Chrissy a casual peck on the cheek. In the car, Chrissy practically leapt into the backseat, so Caroline could sit in the front with Travis, and as soon as they pulled up in front of the loft, she hopped out, leaving them alone.

"Now I know where you live," Travis said to Caroline. "Can I have your phone number as well? I'd like to call you."

"Sure ... okay," Caroline replied. She wrote their number on the inside cover of a book of matches Travis handed her, feeling like a character in a movie. When she gave him back the matches, his hand briefly touched hers. Caroline felt her face turn red. "Thanks for the ride home," she said in a weak voice. " And thanks for a fun night."

"I should be thanking you," Travis insisted, his own voice low. "I'll call you," he promised.

"Great," she said, still blushing. "So long."

"'Bye, Caroline. Nice meeting you, Chrissy," he called out to where Chrissy was waiting in the shadows of the streetlights.

Before the car had even pulled away from the curb Chrissy was needling Caroline. "Still no sparks?" she said skeptically.

"No sparks," Caroline said firmly. "Really, Chrissy. Take my word for it!"

"But he's going to call you, isn't he?" Chrissy

asked her as the elevator lurched upwards. "Will you go out with him if he asks you?"

"Probably."

Chrissy watched Caroline, waiting for more. When it didn't come, she just gave her cousin a maternal pat on the shoulder. "I think it would be a good idea," she said meaningfully. "You know, after . . ."

Caroline finished the sentence silently. *After Luke,* she thought. Yes, after breaking things off with Luke, it probably was healthy to date other people. And she had to admit that being sought after by another guy had definitely given her ego a boost. Caroline was flattered—Travis was smart, attractive, and fun. She couldn't have asked for more. But another part of her almost wished she hadn't met Travis at the Limelight. It was one thing to think about seeing someone new; another thing altogether to go through with it.

Chapter 8

Caroline stretched out lazily on the couch, savoring her plain yogurt and sliced peaches with Grapenuts while she watched a movie on TV. The movie was typical Saturday morning fare—a black-and-white family classic starring Lassie. Caroline felt that she probably should have been in more of a hurry to get up and dressed and out of the apartment, but it felt good to lounge around after being out so late the night before. And besides, it was a little bit quiet and lonely, with Chrissy already out on the *Heart Throb* story shoot. Caroline still hadn't decided how she would spend her free day on her own.

Finished with her breakfast, Caroline wandered back into the kitchen to make a cup of coffee. There was a note from Chrissy pinned to the fridge with a magnet:

Cara, I might be late (especially if the Bonducci Brothers ask me to join their band!) so don't wait for me to have dinner. Have a great day!

Chrissy was accompanying her boss Sophie and *Heart Throb*'s music editor to New Jersey to interview an up-and-coming garage band. Chrissy had been deliriously excited at the prospect of meeting some real rock stars, and Caroline smiled, imagining her cousin throwing aside her internship and college plans to learn how to play the bass guitar.

Caroline was just stepping out of the bathroom after a long, hot shower that had left her fingers looking like elongated prunes when the phone rang. She picked it up with a smile on her face, expecting her parents or one of her friends from San Francisco. Instead, she was greeted by a vaguely familiar male voice.

"May I speak to Caroline Kirby?" the voice asked politely.

"This is Caroline," she answered tentatively.

The voice warmed with pleasure. "This is Travis Merrill. I'm glad I caught you at home!"

"Oh, hi, Travis!" Caroline was surprised to hear the eagerness in her own voice. "I didn't expect to hear from you again this soon."

He laughed. "I know. I said I'd call—I just didn't say I'd call within twelve hours! But the reason is, I have a free evening tonight and I was hoping you might be free, too. I was thinking maybe we could do something together."

Caroline's mind was spinning and the palm of her hand that was clutching the receiver was damp. She was glad Travis had called as he promised he would, but she wished she'd had a little more time to think things over. For a moment Caroline didn't say anything and there was an awkward pause in the conversation. Then suddenly she realized she did want to see Travis again. *What do I need to think things over for? There is nothing to think over. Of course I'm free,* she thought. Luke was just a memory and Travis was a real person—an attractive, interesting person, just the kind of guy she'd been hoping to meet in New York. She'd be crazy to turn him down.

"Travis, I'd love to go out tonight," Caroline said earnestly, hoping her hesitation hadn't been too obvious.

"Fantastic!" he exclaimed. "This is what I had in mind." Travis's plan was to call a theater on Broadway where a hit musical was currently playing to see if there were still tickets available for that night's performance. "I'll pick you up at six, okay? We can get something to eat beforehand. I can never wait until after the show for dinner."

"Me, neither," Caroline admitted. "I'll see you at six then!"

"I'm looking forward to it," Travis said sincerely.

"'Bye."

Caroline hung up the phone feeling giddy. Tucking her towel more snugly around her, she pirouetted to the bedroom. One thing was for sure. She wasn't going to miss Chrissy's company for dinner after all!

Dressed in a short, softly pleated silk skirt and matching jacket, Caroline sat by the open window at the front of the loft, pretending she wasn't keeping an eye out for Travis. It had turned out to be a beautiful afternoon. The day had started out with low clouds and rain, and she had spent most of it inside at various museums. The bad weather had finally been blown aside by the northwest wind and now the sky was crystal-clear. The air smelled almost pure, and Caroline guessed it would be a cool, star-filled night. Perfect for romance, she thought, even though, as she reminded herself, she wasn't necessarily *looking* for romance.

Travis was punctual, ringing the buzzer exactly at six. Caroline met him on the sidewalk, and he ushered her into a waiting cab. "Change in plans," he informed her with a mischievous tilt to his smile. "We're going to take a detour before dinner. I hope you don't mind."

Caroline raised her eyebrows, smiling back. "No, I don't mind, but I am curious."

Travis grinned. "You'll find out soon enough." He asked the driver to take them to Central Park.

"Central Park?" Caroline echoed, tipping her head to one side. "Are we having a picnic in the park?"

Travis just grinned again, his green eyes crinkling at the corners. "I'm not giving any more hints. It's supposed to be a surprise!"

Caroline surprised herself by not becoming at all tongue-tied during the ride to the park. She felt like she'd known Travis for a lot longer than just a day. He was an amusing talker, but he didn't dominate the conversation. He asked questions that got her talking, too.

The driver dropped them off at the south border of Central Park. As Caroline stepped onto the sidewalk, the wind whipped her skirt around her legs and her loose hair across her face. She laughed. "We should have brought kites. We could have gone for a real ride!"

"How 'bout taking a carriage instead?" Travis was pointing and Caroline turned to face a row of horse-drawn carriages, lined up along the curb at the entrance to the park waiting to be hired. Travis watched her expression change from puzzlement to delight. "Go ahead," he urged. "Pick one out!"

Caroline chose a large chestnut horse that reminded her of Chrissy's mare in Iowa, the only other horse she'd ever known personally. A minute later they were settled in the carriage, facing backward, as the horse clopped into the park. "This is the best surprise!" Caroline told Travis, her blue eyes glowing. "I mean it. I can't imagine a better way to see New York on an evening like this."

"That's what I thought!" Travis was clearly pleased that his idea had gone over so well. "This is one of those things I always wanted to do but never would've gotten around to doing on my own. Showing the sights to you was a good excuse."

For a few minutes, Caroline and Travis didn't talk but just enjoyed the sensation of coasting through Central Park high above the ground in the open air. With every stride of the horse Caroline felt more and more relaxed. The past busy week at the U.N. seemed to fade into nothing. She felt a million miles away from her desk in the French translators' offices, from the loft, the museums, the general hustle and bustle of the city. There was traffic speeding by the carriage on the main route through the park, but they were floating above it, immersed in the green of the tree-filled park and the sweet scent of the breeze.

The half hour ride was over much too soon. "We'll have to have another ride soon, under the stars next time," Travis said, giving Caroline a meaningful gaze. Caroline didn't know what to say. She turned to give the chestnut mare one last pat. "But hey," Travis said, in a lighter tone.

"We'd better get moving if we want to eat before the show!"

They only had time for sandwiches before they had to make their way to Broadway and the Uris Theater. Travis had been able to get tickets to the musical after all, and even though they weren't the best seats in the house, the show was wonderful. Caroline came out singing. "It's been awhile since I've seen a real musical," she explained. "At home we mostly go to the opera and the symphony. Actually, my last experience of a musical was onstage in a performance of *Oklahoma!* at my high school!"

Travis looked impressed. "I bet you were what's-her-name, the one Mrs. Partridge Family, Shirley Jones, played in the movie."

Caroline shook her head. "No way. I was just in the chorus, and the only reason I got *that* part was because I had a lot of dance training because of my ballet."

They were in yet another taxi, this time heading back downtown to SoHo. Without thinking about it, Caroline found herself confiding to Travis about how dedicated she'd been to ballet, and what a difficult decision it had been to give it up. "I realized I didn't want to make ballet my life. I had to give up so much when I was studying it. Actually, *Oklahoma!* was one of the first activities I got involved in after I quit." Caroline told Travis how jealous she'd been of her cousin when Chrissy received the dance solo in *Oklahoma!* instead of her.

"I can't picture you two clashing," Travis said with a skeptical smile. "You seemed like you were getting along pretty well last night."

Caroline shook her head. "Boy, you should see us sometimes! We're like night and day in some respects. At first when she moved in with my family I never thought we'd survive living together. But now she's really my best friend, even when we disagree." Talking about Chrissy made Caroline wonder if her cousin would be home yet from her day on location with *Heart Throb*. Then she started thinking about what she should do when the taxi pulled up at the loft. Invite Travis upstairs? If Chrissy were at home, it could be fun. Harmless. If not . . .

Caroline wasn't sure if she was ready to be alone—*really* alone—with Travis. But when the cab stopped, she didn't get a chance to say anything. Travis quickly paid the driver and before Caroline knew what had happened, she and Travis were standing alone on the sidewalk underneath a street lamp as the cab roared off to look for another fare.

Caroline felt her face flood with color. It seemed as if Travis had assumed he'd be asked up for a while. The realization made her tremble, half with panic and half in anticipation.

Travis must have read the embarrassed confusion in Caroline's expression. He hurried to reassure her. "Hey, I'm not going to force my way up to your apartment, I promise," he said, running a hand through his hair.

"I am kind of tired . . . ," Caroline began, by way of an excuse.

"Me, too," Travis said easily. "I just wanted a chance to say good night to you without an audience."

Caroline smiled. "I know. It sort of cramps your style when the meter's running and the cabbie's tapping his fingers impatiently on the steering wheel!" She spoke lightly, but her palms were sweating a little from nervousness. She knew what was coming; she could tell by the warm, serious look in Travis's green eyes that he wanted to kiss her.

"So." He put his hands in the pockets of his trousers and rocked back on his heels, also sounding more confident than he looked. "Maybe I can see you again?"

Caroline nodded. "I had a really nice time tonight, Travis. Thanks for everything," she said softly.

"It was my pleasure," Travis insisted. "Really. So . . ." His voice trailed off in a questioning fashion.

"So . . ." Caroline echoed.

They stood in silence for a few seconds. Around them, the summer night was suddenly still. The full moon shone down on them, even brighter than the streetlamp. Then Travis stepped forward and placed his hands awkwardly on Caroline's shoulders. When she didn't resist, he leaned down and brushed her lips with his own. His kiss was tentative at first, and then more firm as Caroline found herself responding eagerly. Despite her doubts about her true feelings for him, she was excited by Travis's nearness. He was cute. And very nice. And his kiss felt so wonderful . . . Caroline closed her eyes.

Suddenly the city became a peaceful country field, and the boy with his arms around her was Luke. She forced her eyes open and focused on Travis in an effort to push the memory out of her mind.

After a long moment Travis pulled away reluctantly. He brushed the hair off Caroline's forehead with a gentle touch before he let her go. "Good night, Caroline," he said in a low voice. "I'll call you again. Soon."

Caroline hoped it wouldn't be *too* soon. This time she did feel like she needed more than twelve hours to think about things. "Good night. Thanks again!"

Travis jogged off to the corner to hail another cab and Caroline, her legs still a little wobbly from his kiss, unlocked the door to the entryway of her building. Travis turned to wave at her as she let herself in. Riding to the loft in the elevator, Caroline was half relieved that Travis had left and half regretful that she hadn't asked him up for a while. Kissing him had been fantastic, definitely worth a repeat. When she found the loft dark and another note from Chrissy stuck on the refrigerator—*Came home to change and then went out again with friends from work. See you at bedtime!*—she started to feel mad at herself. The only reason she didn't invite Travis up, didn't enjoy his good-night kiss more, was because the whole time she was still thinking about Luke. Luke, who was probably out on a big Saturday-Night-in-Danbury Date with his new girlfriend!

How pathetic, Caroline thought disgustedly as she kicked off her heels and peeled off her stockings. *This is the last time, the absolute final time, I let him get in between me and my fun! Next time I'm out with Travis or any other guy, we'll be dancing—and kissing—until dawn!*

Having made this resolution, Caroline felt better. But as she crossed the living room floor to the TV, her eyes were diverted by the telephone. Without really thinking, she picked it up. It wouldn't hurt to dial the Mastersons' number, one last time. She could prove to herself that Luke wasn't home, that he wasn't wasting his time thinking about her.

Slowly, Caroline punched in the numbers with her fingers. The phone rang three times and then a deep voice said hello in that Midwestern twang of Luke's that she'd always found so adorable. She hung up, her hands shaking. For a moment, a very brief moment, Luke had seemed so close. But Caroline knew it had just been an illusion.

She decided not to watch TV. Gathering up her hose and shoes, she drifted into the bedroom to undress. All of a sudden, she was too tired to wait up for Chrissy. She wasn't up to answering

Chrissy's dozens of questions about her date and
what she thought about Travis, especially as she
didn't know the answer to that particular question herself.

Chapter 9

"Finally!" Chrissy hollered at her cousin as Caroline stepped off the elevator into the living room. "I thought you were never going to show up! Hurry up and change! We're going to be late!"

"Whoa, I'm sorry!" Caroline lifted her hands palms up in a gesture of helplessness. "I had to work a little late. Chrissy, you should have seen me—I got to sit in the translator's booth with Juliet and listen in on an actual U.N. session! Juliet was phenomenal. She was translating from French to English *simultaneously*, right while the guy was taking—"

"I don't want to hear about it now," Chrissy said impatiently. She was wearing her new red dress, clutching a sequined purse, and dancing up and down as if she had ants in her pantyhose.

"Do you want to miss the premiere of Tom Cruise's new movie?"

"Okay, okay! I'm hurrying." Caroline disappeared into the bedroom. Chrissy followed in time to see her dive into the walk-in closet. Five minutes later Caroline was dressed except for shoes and jewelry. "Now was that fast, or was that fast?" she asked Chrissy as she slipped on a pair of long onyx earrings.

"That was fast," Chrissy admitted, looking nervously at her watch. "But, Cara, we're still running ten minutes late. . . ."

"We'll get there," Caroline promised, plunging into the closet again to find her black patent leather pumps. "Oh, Chrissy. I almost forgot to tell you!" she exclaimed, popping her head back out. "Guess where we're invited a week from Monday?"

Chrissy shrugged, drawing a blank. It had to have something to do with Caroline's internship. She took a stab in the dark. "Um, Paris?"

"No. A formal cocktail party at the U.N.!"

Chrissy was interested. "Will there be, like, foreign *celebrities* there?" she asked, her eyes lighting up.

"Well, they won't be celebrities exactly," Caroline said. "There *will* be diplomats attending, and"—Caroline paused for effect—"visiting royalty."

"Oh, wow!" Chrissy clapped her hands together like a child who'd just been given an unexpected present. "You mean like Princess

Diana and Prince Charles and Fergie?"

"Well, probably not them." Caroline had a sudden terrible vision of Chrissy bolting up to Queen Elizabeth and giving her a big farm-style hug. Maybe bringing Chrissy along to an ultraformal U.N. reception wasn't going to be such a good idea after all. But she really owed Chrissy one, especially since their invitations to the movie premiere tonight were courtesy of *Heart Throb*.

"No, probably not them," Caroline repeated, "but I promise you at least a dozen other assorted king and sheik types. Juliet said most likely Prince Albert of Monaco will put in an appearance. And unlike Prince Charles, he's single!"

"All right!" Chrissy giggled. "Wait till I call home. 'Guess what, Mom and Dad. I'm going to be a princess!'"

As they were about to step into the elevator, Chrissy slapped a hand to her forehead and sprinted back to the bedroom. She returned a moment later with a handful of tiny notepads and two ballpoint pens which she proceeded to stuff into her already bulging sequined clutch.

"What's all that for?" asked Caroline, turning the key and directing the elevator to the first floor.

"Sophie wants me to take notes tonight during the movie—I mean, the *film*." Chrissy adopted an upper-crust accent. "Tomorrow at work we'll talk about it, and if she decides to use any of my observations, I'll actually get my name at the top of the article along with hers!"

"That's great," Caroline said, genuinely impressed. "But, Chrissy," she added in a teasing tone, "if you have to concentrate on taking notes the whole time, you won't be able to scope the stars!"

Chrissy frowned. "I hadn't thought about that," she confessed seriously. Then she tossed her long blond hair over one shoulder and smiled. "But don't worry. I'll find a way to do both!"

They walked to the end of their block and Chrissy stepped into the street. By now she was an expert at flagging down taxis. "A skill that'll really come in handy back in Danbury," she joked to Caroline as they entered a dilapidated cab that must have had a couple hundred thousand miles on it. "Oh, and that reminds me. Something else I almost forgot! Travis called."

"*That* reminds you?" Caroline bristled. "Danbury reminds you that Travis called?"

"Well, sort of." Chrissy shrugged apologetically. "Don't be so sensitive, Cara. I didn't mean it the way it sounded. I mean, Luke is Luke and Travis is Travis and—"

"Did he leave a message?" Caroline interrupted Chrissy's well-intentioned but garbled attempt at an explanation.

"He just said to let you know he called. I told him we were going out tonight and to call back tomorrow." Chrissy peered at Caroline, trying to read her expression. "That was the right thing to do, wasn't it? You're not trying to blow him off or anything, are you?"

"Yes, it was and no, I'm not," Caroline affirmed. She was just going to drop the subject at that, but then she recalled all the other times when she had kept her troubles to herself. In the end, it had always turned out better when she had shared her problems with her cousin. Chrissy was a caring friend and right then Caroline felt as if she could use some of her solid, homegrown advice. "Oh, Chrissy, I don't know. I had a good time with him the other night—a really good time. I mean, when he kissed me good night"— Caroline flushed slightly—"there were really some fireworks. But for some reason afterwards I felt guilty, like I'd cheated on Luke or something. And we're not even going out anymore! Isn't that ridiculous?"

"You can't expect things to feel completely right with the first person you meet after Luke, you know," Chrissy reminded her gently. "Maybe Travis came along too soon. There'll be other guys."

"But I want to have fun *now*." Caroline snapped open her purse emphatically. She pulled out a lipstick and waved it at Chrissy. "I want to forget all about Luke. Being with Travis just wasn't enough to do it. Just when I'd be feeling free, Luke would come popping back into my head."

"Believe me, I know what that's like. It just takes time, that's all." Chrissy smiled mischievously. "A handsome movie star at the premiere tonight might be looking for a gorgeous female escort. I bet you forget Luke in about a millisecond then!"

Their taxi approached the theater, where an enormous, neon-bright marquee announced Tom Cruise and the premiere of his latest movie. Chrissy and Caroline both held their breath as the driver pulled up behind a row of long, dark limousines. Men in tuxedos and women in satin and sequins were stepping out to the glare of camera flashbulbs.

"I fell like I'm at the Academy Awards or something," Chrissy whispered, her blue eyes wide with awe.

"Me, too," Caroline admitted. "Well, I guess we'd better pay our fare. We can't hide in the cab all night!"

Showing their invitations, they walked quickly into the theater past a row of stern-looking doormen. Chrissy was a little disappointed that none of the photographers tried to take her picture. They could have mistaken her for a minor soap-opera star at least!

Inside the theater, instead of popcorn and soda, elegantly dressed waiters were serving tall, flutelike glasses of bubbling champagne. Chrissy and Caroline presented their tickets again and were escorted to their seats. Chrissy nearly got dizzy looking rapidly from side to side as they strolled down the aisle. She was sure she saw Bill Cosby on the left and then Cher on the right. She dug into Caroline's side with her elbow. "Cara," she hissed, in what sounded to her cousin like the loudest whisper in the history of the world. "Look! It's Rob Lowe!"

"Chrissy, shh!" Caroline whispered back, ducking gratefully into their row. "Let's sit down and *then* point and stare!"

Sophie was already in her seat and she greeted the cousins with a warm smile. "You must be Caroline. Chrissy's told me a lot about you. I'm glad you could make it tonight!"

Caroline shook Sophie's hand as she lowered herself into the plush chair. "It's very nice to meet you, Sophie. Thank you so much for the extra ticket!"

Chrissy was leaning over Caroline to get Sophie's attention. "Sophie, you were right. There are a million famous people here! This is great."

Sophie pointed to the pad and pencil she'd tucked under her left thigh. "Just don't forget to watch the film," she cautioned, her eyes twinkling. "We want to go home with a movie review, not a who-was-with-who-and-wearing-what review!"

Caroline had glanced back toward the aisle when Chrissy and Sophie started talking. Now she jumped halfway out of her seat despite her resolution to be dignified. "Johnny Carson! And there's Bruce Willis and Demi Moore!" she said to Chrissy in an excited whisper.

Chrissy had spotted Jacqueline Bissett and Alexander Godunov. "Holy mazoly, he's even handsomer than his pictures," she breathed.

Too soon, the lights dimmed and the movie began. The story was fast moving and very funny, and Caroline was amazed at Chrissy's self control. She didn't just sit back and enjoy herself, but watched attentively, bending forward every few minutes to jot something down. Sophie, in contrast, seemed to write almost constantly, but somehow without ever taking her eyes off the screen.

When the lights came up again, the audience rose as one in a standing ovation. "There's a short reception now and then the real big wigs—that's not us—will leave for a private party," Sophie informed Chrissy and Caroline, who were applauding with all their might. "I want to introduce you to a few people, Chrissy, so don't get lost."

The moment the three joined the flood of people moving towards the lobby, however, they were separated. Caroline saw Chrissy being propelled in one direction and Sophie in another and after a brief hesitation, hurried after her cousin.

"Where's Sophie?" Chrissy asked her, looking around anxiously.

"She went that way." Caroline nodded into the glittering crowd. "I think."

"Great!" Chrissy moaned. "Now I'm not going to meet any celebrities or movie critics." Then she grabbed Caroline's arm and squeezed it so hard Caroline yelped. "There he is!" Chrissy squealed.

"There who is?" Caroline asked, shaking off

Chrissy's hand and rubbing her pinched arm.

"The man of the hour—Tom Cruise!" Caroline followed Chrissy's adoring gaze. Tom Cruise, looking more real but just as gorgeous as he had on screen, was standing only a few tantalizing yards away.

"Holy cow," Caroline murmured, borrowing one of Chrissy's pet phrases.

"C'mon, let's go introduce ourselves!" Chrissy grabbed Caroline's arm again and started forward eagerly.

"Absolutely not!" Caroline vetoed the proposition vehemently. "Haven't you ever heard of admiring from a distance, Chrissy? You do not just march up to Tom Cruise at his own movie premiere and say, 'Hi, how's it going?' At least, not if you're a nobody like us!"

Chrissy stopped obediently but she made a pouting face. "Don't be a wet blanket, Cara. Oh, look, he's leaving! This is our last chance!"

This time Caroline wasn't able to shake free of Chrissy's grip. It would have required a real wrestling match and the less attention they drew to themselves, she figured, the better. It was embarrassing enough to be seen sprinting through the elegant crowd. She only hoped it wasn't too obvious that they were in hot pursuit of Tom Cruise.

On her way to the exit, Chrissy nearly ran into a waiter with a full tray. They hit the sidewalk just as Tom Cruise and an unidentified woman slipped into a waiting limousine. "Oh, well," Caroline said lightly, exhaling with relief. "He got away from us. Let's go back inside and see if we can find your boss."

"You give up too easily!" Chrissy was still pulling Caroline down the walk toward the curb. "But I have an idea!" Waving her free arm wildly, Chrissy managed to stop the next taxi coming down the street.

"But what about Sophie?" Caroline asked. "We'd better go look for her."

"She'll understand," Chrissy replied. She ducked into the cab, leaving Caroline no choice but to follow.

"Follow that limo!" she instructed the driver breathlessly, sounding like a corny detective in an old movie.

The driver was young, and luckily, judging from the broad smile he flashed Chrissy, he seemed to have a sense of humor. "If you've got the dough, I'll take you anywhere," he promised them gallantly. With a screech of tires, the cab whipped back into traffic. By dodging a few cars, the driver managed to pull up behind the limousine at the next stoplight.

Caroline, meanwhile, was gaping at her cousin in complete disbelief. "You've finally lost it," she said grimly. "This is too much. We're chasing Tom Cruise's limo in a taxi. What do you plan to do if we actually catch him?"

Chrissy crossed her arms over her chest, smiling like the cat that swallowed the canary. "I told you I had an idea, and it's a really good one." She patted her purse. "I'll pretend I'm authorized to request an interview with him for *Heart Throb!* I do have a company ID with my picture on it, so I can prove I'm not just an autograph hound. Clever, huh?"

Caroline groaned. *Leave it to Chrissy,* she thought, but she couldn't help smiling and enjoying the adventure. "If you pull this off, Chrissy, I'll make your bed every day for our whole four years of college."

Just then the driver swerved sharply into the left lane to make an abrupt turn as the light was turning red. Caroline was flung against Chrissy and both girls squealed. "Sorry, ladies," the driver said smoothly. "But I think their driver's on to us. He was cruising along just fine and then out of nowhere he pulled a fast one. Hold onto your hats!"

The driver floored it, and Chrissy and Caroline cheered wildly. A block later they were back on the tail of the limousine, speeding up First Avenue. "I feel like I fell asleep and woke up in the middle of a *Starsky and Hutch* rerun!" Chrissy shouted at Caroline happily. But their success didn't hold out for long. This time the limo pulled a U-turn at a corner, and before the taxi could do the same another car drew up beside it, blocking the way.

"Shoot!" Chrissy exclaimed, twisting in her seat to peer after the limo as it made its escape.

The driver beat his palm against the steering wheel, as disappointed as she was. "Aw, I'm sorry," he said, sounding like he meant it. "We almost had 'em. Where to now?"

Chrissy slumped back against the seat, her expression forlorn. "I guess we might as well go home," she said with a sigh.

Caroline gave the address and the driver swung around the block in order to head back downtown. Then she tried to tease a smile back onto her cousin's face. "We could stop back at the theater and see if we could find another movie star to follow," she suggested jokingly.

Chrissy sat bolt upright, staring at Caroline with a glint in her eye. "Hey, good idea, Cara!" Then she started to giggle. "We almost had 'em," she said, echoing the cab driver's lament. "Oh, boy, we almost had 'em!"

"Now that's what I call dedicated journalism!" Caroline remarked, laughing. "Maybe Sophie will give you a promotion."

"New York is great!" Chrissy exclaimed, flashing Caroline a breezy smile. "Wouldn't you rather be right here than anywhere else in the world, Cara?"

Caroline nodded emphatically. "You better believe it!"

Chapter 10

"Travis called *again*," Chrissy greeted Caroline as her cousin dropped her briefcase next to the elevator and made a mad dash for the refrigerator.

"He did?" Caroline pretended to be surprised as she snapped the tab on an icy can of diet soda.

Chrissy smoothed the skirt of her long-waisted cotton dress. She had only just gotten home from work herself. She gave Caroline a skeptical look. "C'mon, Cara, don't act so innocent! I've given you a couple of messages and you know he's going to keep calling until he reaches you." Chrissy's expression became mischievous. "If you don't call him back this time, next time *I* talk to him I'm going to give him your phone number at the U.N.!"

"I know I should call him back," Caroline admitted as she hitched herself up onto one of the high stools along the kitchen counter. She sighed. "It would be fun to see him again. Maybe we could double with Kirk . . . ."

Chrissy snorted. "Yeah, Kirk was real interested in me. You notice how *he's* been ringing the phone off the hook lately!"

Caroline giggled. "It was just a thought."

"You really don't want to be alone with Travis?" Chrissy asked as she pulled a bottle of cherry-flavored seltzer out of the refrigerator. She shook her head and whistled, unbelieving. "Personally, I think you're crazy. He's pretty darn cute. And, you know, he's not going to wait around indefinitely. Someone else will snap him up if you don't. Hey! I've got an idea!"

Caroline recognized Chrissy's expression of sudden inspiration. It meant she was about to be let in on a harebrained scheme she wouldn't want anything to do with. "What?" she said, prepared for the worst.

"We're meeting Rachel and the gang from *Heart Throb* in Little Italy later, right? To go to that festival thing Rachel told us about. Why don't we call Travis and Kirk and ask them to come along, too?"

Chrissy made it sound so simple. A casual group outing—nothing that could lead to an uncomfortable situation. Still, Caroline hesitated. "I don't think so," she said finally. "I'll call him tonight when we get home—"

"Yeah, right." Chrissy rolled her eyes and shook her loose blond hair. "You mean you'll conveniently forget to call him tonight and I'll get stuck taking his call again tomorrow! Unh-uh. Get on the phone right this minute, young lady!'"

Caroline walked toward the phone, dragging her feet. She picked up the receiver and, referring to the message Chrissy had written on a piece of brown paper bag, dialed Travis's number. All except the last digit, that is. Caroline pretended to be waiting while the phone rang, and then after a suitable interval she hung up. "Nobody home," she informed Chrissy in a cheerful voice.

"That's funny," Chrissy observed, puzzled. "He only called about five minutes before you walked in, and he said he'd be around for the rest of the evening. Did you read the number right?" She held out her hand for the phone. "Here, let me try."

Caroline was cornered. "I didn't dial the whole number," she confessed. "Oh, Chrissy, I just don't want to see him tonight, okay? Can't we just leave it at that?"

"Sure." Chrissy's cornflower blue eyes grew warm with concern. "I didn't mean to be bossy. I was just trying to help. But it's up to you."

"I know it is. And thanks," Caroline said sincerely.

She polished off her soda and then, retrieving her briefcase, crossed to the bedroom and flopped down on her bed, her cousin following.

"Good idea," Chrissy said, taking a swan dive onto her own bed. "We can lie down for a few minutes before we go to Little Italy."

"A few minutes?" Caroline looked sleepily at the clock. "I was thinking more like a few hours. It's only six, and we're not meeting those guys until eight."

"But we've never been to Little Italy and I was hoping we could walk over early and look around for a while on our own." Chrissy was giving her cousin the lost-puppy-dog look Caroline always found impossible to resist. "It's such a nice night, and we only have a week and a half left in New York. . . ."

"All right, you win," Caroline agreed good-naturedly. "I'm just going to close my eyes for a sec."

"I'll wake you up if you fall asleep," Chrissy promised.

"Gee, thanks!"

Once they'd changed into comfortable clothes and shoes and were back outside strolling along the sunlit sidewalk, Caroline felt more energetic. If Chrissy loved early morning, late afternoon was Caroline's favorite time of day. Almost everyone they passed on the sidewalk wore the same light-hearted expression. Work was over and the long summer evening stretched out before them. The whole world, young and old, was out on the street—walking, jogging, sitting on park benches, hanging out on corners. An open fire hydrant had attracted a dozen little kids who were splashing and shouting in the cold spray. A young man with a beard was playing the violin, the case to his instrument lying open on the sidewalk for people to throw money in. The cafes were all crowded, with customers packed into the little tables on the sidewalk.

"Don't you love New York?" Chrissy and Caroline said to each other at the same time. They both laughed.

"Seriously," Caroline continued. "I'm so glad Roy Fisher and his band decided to go on tour for a month. If it hadn't been for that, we wouldn't be here."

"I know. We're pretty lucky." They paused to look at the display in a boutique window. Chrissy grimaced at a mannequin wearing an artfully ripped, tie-dyed T-shirt dress, accessorized with random safety pins. "I really feel a little bit like a real New Yorker, even if I'll never wear junk like that."

"Oh, I don't know." Caroline pretended to take the dress seriously. "I think that would be just perfect for a church social back in Danbury!"

Chrissy laughed heartily. "Can you imagine? Everyone back home thinks I'm nuts enough as it is since I went to live with you in California!"

They continued on down the sidewalk, dodging a couple of kids on psychedelic-colored skateboards. "By the way," Caroline said, "I've been so preoccupied with avoiding Travis's phone calls that I forgot to ask how your call home went last night." She knew Chrissy had been thinking, and worrying a lot about her family lately. "How is everybody?"

"Not bad," Chrissy answered, her eyes brightening. "Actually, I was sort of surprised! I'd been getting depressed in my own mind about things at home, but Mom and Dad sound pretty positive. Mom actually likes her job as a cashier, can you believe it?"

Caroline couldn't, but she didn't say as much. She just nodded, encouraging Chrissy to keep talking. "She says absolutely everybody comes in the store—she's never been so on top of Danbury gossip. And the corn is getting tall, the weather's been perfect . . . . I guess all that's left for anyone to do is cross their fingers."

"I'm glad," Caroline said, with genuine feeling. Having grown up in the city, Caroline had been completely ignorant about life on a farm until she'd spent that spring break with Chrissy's family. The visit had been a real eye-opener. Caroline had left with a real appreciation of how hard people like the Maddens worked to hold onto farms and homes that had been in their families for generations. "Any . . . other news?" she asked, hinting delicately.

"Not really," Chrissy said breezily, missing the hint altogether at first. Then she caught sight of Caroline's crestfallen expression. "Oh, you mean about Luke? Why didn't you just come right out and say so? My dad says he's been getting a lot of crop-dusting jobs."

"That's all?"

"Well, and my mother's seen him a few times in the store."

"Oh." Caroline didn't know what she'd expected to hear. That Luke had been asking about her? Fat chance!

"And *oh*!" Chrissy exclaimed loudly as an afterthought hit her. Caroline jumped. "My mom did tell me that *Ben*"—Chrissy spoke the name with emphatic distaste—"is hot and heavy as ever with his new steady. In fact, she came in the store the other day and my mom said she was wearing *somebody's* class ring on a chain around her neck, for the whole world to see!" Caroline stifled a smile. That was obviously the boldest move a girl could make in Danbury, Iowa. "Boy, Cara, were you ever on target," Chrissy continued righteously, "when you said those farm boys were for the birds!"

"I was? I did?" Caroline asked weakly.

"Yes, sirree. I for one can't wait to get to college and meet some *real* men!"

"Me, neither," Caroline agreed, but she didn't really feel it. She might as well keep talking as if she wasn't still hung up on Luke. Maybe eventually she'd talk herself into believing it.

They had a free hour to spend before they were supposed to meet Rachel and the three *Heart Throb* interns Chrissy liked to hang around with. So Chrissy and Caroline wandered the neighborhoods of Little Italy, admiring the decorations for the festival of San Gennaro, and drooling over the luscious cream-filled pastries displayed in the bakery windows. Chrissy finally gave in to temptation and sampled a few, assuring Caroline that by the time they got around to eating dinner she'd have plenty of room for platefuls of pasta.

The restaurant Rachel had suggested as a meeting place was called Alessandro's. Chrissy and Caroline strolled up to find Jackie, Bernard, and José already enjoying drinks at an outdoor table topped with a red-, green-, and white-striped umbrella. The three greeted the cousins with grins.

José waved a loaf of Italian bread. "Hurry up before we eat it all!" he threatened Chrissy.

Chrissy introduced Caroline to her coworkers, watching her cousin's expression for a reaction. Caroline was always trying to make her more worldly and sophisticated; Chrissy thought she should certainly approve of her interesting new friends. Jackie was a glamorous city girl, born and raised in New York. She was the sort of person who would actually buy the torn dress with the safety pins in the boutique window. Bernard was also very New York and very chic. He went to NYU, where he was studying cinematography. And José came all the way from Madrid.

Caroline did seem impressed, by their friendliness if nothing else. The group chatted for a few moments, waiting for Rachel before they ordered dinner.

Suddenly Jackie turned to Caroline, her dark-shadowed eyes curious and sympathetic. "I don't mean to pry, but Chrissy told me that you're having a hard time getting over your old boyfriend."

Caroline darted an accusing look at Chrissy, who simultaneously kicked Jackie under the table. Jackie looked surprised. Chrissy knew she couldn't blame her new friend for being her usual outspoken self. It was her own fault for blabbing about Caroline's deepest, darkest secrets at lunch with the other interns that day. "Um, Caroline's actually plenty over him now," Chrissy said quickly as she searched her brain for a way to change the subject. "She has other guys calling her all the time and—"

"That's okay, Chrissy!" Caroline snapped. Then she laughed ruefully. "I mean, we might as well keep the story straight. Jackie's closer to the truth than you are!"

"Well, I've been there myself," Jackie assured Caroline, tapping a long magenta fingernail on her glass for emphasis. "Three boyfriends ago, I just had the toughest time of it. He was something. He was really hot."

Caroline raised one eyebrow. Three boyfriends ago? Luke was only her second, total!

Meanwhile Bernard had reached across the table to pat Caroline's hand. "Breaking up's the worst," he commiserated. "It seems like you only ever have two options. Either tell yourself you're going to forget him and get out there and have the wildest, craziest time you can, and you probably *will* forget him, or else admit to yourself that

you want him back. Give in. Call him and tell
him."

Ordinarily Caroline would resent having her
personal life discussed like this, but these people
were Chrissy's friends and they seemed to consider themselves her friends as well. She took a
deep breath and tried to be tolerant. "I'm sort of
wavering between those two options," she told
Bernard shyly.

Then out of the corner of her eye Caroline spotted Rachel weaving her way toward their table.
Before she greeted her friend, relieved to have
an excuse to direct the conversation away from
herself, Caroline sent a harsh whisper in Chrissy's
direction. "You're in for it," she hissed at her
cousin, who was cowering behind her tall glass of
iced tea.

Dinner was delicious and extremely filling.
Even Caroline ate enormous amounts of pasta in
various rich sauces, and as they paid the bill she
swapped jokes with the others about having to be
rolled down the sidewalk. The street festival was
in full swing by the time they wandered up. The
narrow street had been blocked off and dozens of
booths set up. The strings of colored bulbs illumi-
nated games of chance, concession stands, musicians, fortune-tellers, and, unbelievably, a Ferris
wheel pressed in between two apartment buildings in a vacant lot. The others howled with
laughter at one booth where Chrissy and Jackie
performed in front of a video camera, lip-
synching to a popular song by the Bangles. For a

few dollars each they could buy the tape, their very own music video. Chrissy waved it triumphantly. "Think MTV will be interested?" she joked. Caroline and Rachel browsed at a display of costume jewelry, finally giving in and buying a pair of earrings each, while Chrissy bought a water pistol for her little brother at a booth selling toys.

They regrouped at the Ferris wheel. "Okay, everybody up!" Chrissy ordered. "No one better chicken out. This is only half the size of the Ferris wheel at the county fair back home!"

They purchased tickets and lined up, and, as luck would have it, Chrissy and Caroline ended up riding together. They both held their breath as the Ferris wheel swept them upwards, where for a brief moment they could see far beyond the low buildings of Little Italy to the skyscrapers of midtown. As the wheel headed down, Chrissy looked guiltily at Caroline. "Okay, I'm ready," she said. "Go ahead, yell at me for being a blabbermouth and having such nosy friends!"

Caroline made a stern face, but she couldn't hold it. Instead she just laughed. "I *was* pretty mad for a while there," she had to admit, "and I *was* planning on chewing you out. But now I'm not mad anymore. Anyhow, Bernard was right. What's the point of stewing about it? I should just take action either way."

"So, which way?" Chrissy inquired as they swooped upward again, their hair blowing wildly in the wind created by the spinning Ferris wheel.

"That part I'm still not sure about. Maybe I should consult one of the fortune tellers!"

"You know, that's not a bad idea," Chrissy said in all seriousness. "At the last county fair I had my palm read. I should have listened to that Gypsy woman! She told me tall, blond men who drive red pickup trucks weren't to be trusted. Little did I know!"

Caroline laughed grimly. "What about tall, dark-haired guys who fly planes?"

"I can't vouch for those."

They enjoyed the Ferris wheel in silence for a few minutes. Then they could tell by the gradual slowing of the wheel's motion that the ride was nearing an end. "What goes up, must come down. All good things come to an end and all that," Chrissy observed philosophically.

But does it have to happen that way? Caroline wondered to herself.

Chapter 11

It was a rainy Saturday morning, and for once Chrissy followed Caroline's lead and lingered in bed until almost ten. Their last week in New York City was before them; a week from Sunday they would pack their bags and board the plane to Iowa, where Caroline would visit for a few days before continuing to San Francisco. If it hadn't been for the weather, Chrissy would have been up and at 'em early, but her bed was so cozy and warm. . . .

Chrissy had been facing the window, lazily watching the wet branches of the tree in front of the apartment building scrape against the panes. Now she rolled over just in time to see Caroline come to life with a yawn and a stretch.

"Well?" Chrissy asked Caroline eagerly.

"Well what?" Caroline said, her eyes innocent behind her rumpled blond bangs.

"You know!" Chrissy's bed squeaked as she gave an impatient bounce. "I was asleep when you got home. How was it?"

Despite heroic efforts to keep her eyes open, Chrissy had dozed off before Caroline returned from her date the night before. A few days earlier Caroline had finally given in and called Travis. Now Chrissy wanted the full scoop on their date. As Caroline hesitated, Chrissy pressed her. "C'mon, Cara. Tell all!"

"Well . . . It was fun." Caroline curled back up under her comforter, and closed her eyes again.

Chrissy frowned. "Cara, don't you dare go back to sleep! I want the whole truth and nothing but the truth, this instant!"

Caroline giggled. "All right, all right! I was just teasing you. But it *was* fun."

"Details, details!" Chrissy shouted, threatening to start a pillow fight.

"Okay." Caroline put on a businesslike expression. "First, we had dinner at a fantastic Greek restaurant called Estia. It was hilarious. These Greek musicians serenaded us at our table. And the food was amazing."

"I don't care about the food." Chrissy flourished a pillow, grinning. "I want to hear about Travis!"

Caroline smiled slyly. "Well, he looked really good. He was wearing khaki pants and a white shirt and navy blazer and a plaid madras tie. Oh, and he got his hair cut pretty short."

Chrissy tossed the pillow. Caroline managed to ward it off with her arm, even though she was nearly helpless with laughter. "Hold your horses, Chrissy! I'm getting to the good part." She threw the pillow back at her cousin, who caught it easily and lobbed it back. "After dinner we went to this old movie theater that was built around the nineteen twenties and probably looks exactly the same as it did then. They only play old movies and we saw *The Philadelphia Story*. We sat in these seats that didn't have an armrest between them—courting seats, they used to call them."

"And did you . . . *court*?" Chrissy asked, wiggling her blond eyebrows suggestively.

"Sort of," Caroline admitted. "He had his arm around me the whole time."

"That's not what we'd call courting back in Danbury," Chrissy said, disappointed. "You mean you didn't kiss at all?"

"Well, not in the movie theater."

Chrissy looked hopeful. "But later?"

Caroline sighed, no longer joking around. "No, not even later. I mean, we had one of those goodnight pecks in the backseat of the taxi when he dropped me off, but that doesn't really count as *kissing*. See, after the movie we went out for a drink and we talked for hours, literally. That's why I was home so late. I told Travis about Luke and how I just haven't been feeling ready to get romantically involved with someone else. He completely understood. He said he hoped he'd get to see more of me before I leave New York, just to have a good time."

Chrissy nodded. Even if Cara hadn't found true love, it sounded as if she'd made a good friend—and that was pretty good going in Chrissy's book. "How do you feel about it?" she asked in a serious tone.

Caroline sat up in bed, hugging the pillow to her stomach. "Pretty good," she admitted. "Relieved. I'm just not ready for another boyfriend yet. Especially one that lives in New York City when I'll be going to college in Colorado! But dating casually, that's another thing. Now I can look forward to seeing Travis again. I'm not going to put any pressure on myself."

"Gosh, you have it all worked out!" Chrissy was definitely impressed.

"Sounds like it, doesn't it?" Caroline didn't point out that she only had things worked out as far as her friendship with Travis was concerned; her feelings about Luke were as unresolved as ever.

Chrissy sighed, somewhat enviously. "You've had a romantic month in New York, what with Travis falling for you and taking you on glamorous dates and moonlit carriage rides. How come nothing like that happened to me?"

"Well, the month's not over yet," Caroline reminded her. "The day after tomorrow's your big chance." When Chrissy looked blank,

Caroline added, "The diplomatic cocktail party, remember?"

"Oh, yeah!" Chrissy's eyes sparkled. "Maybe a handsome young sheik will invite me to join his harem or something!"

"Anything's possible," Caroline conceded with a grin. "Look at Queen Noor of Jordan. She used to be an ordinary American girl. She went to Princeton!"

Chrissy pictured herself swathed in gauzy Arabian clothing and decked in jewels. As if reading her mind, Caroline suddenly gasped. "Clothes!" she exclaimed, horrified. "What are we going to wear?"

Chrissy didn't see any reason to panic. "Well, I can wear my red dress with the sequins again. And you have a dozen nice dresses in your closet."

"But this is a *formal* cocktail party," Caroline reminded Chrissy haughtily. "You can't wear the same thing you'd wear dancing at the Limelight."

"Well, excuse me!" Chrissy said in a pretend huff. "I'm afraid I don't have anything appropriate in my wardrobe, Queen Noor. I guess I'll have to decline the invitation."

"I didn't mean it that way," Caroline apologized. "Sorry. But you're not the only one—I don't have the right thing to wear, either."

"So, what are we going to do about it?"

"Go out and buy something, I guess."

"Well, I don't know about you, but I've about reached the limit of my spending money,"

Chrissy pointed out. "I didn't exactly work an evening gown into my budget!"

"I wasn't suggesting that we buy Dior originals," Caroline said sensibly. "I was thinking more along the lines of exploring the vintage-clothing shops in Greenwich Village. We could probably pick up a couple of neat secondhand dresses without spending very much." She looked outside. The rain, falling steadily, was like a solid gray curtain pulled closed on the wrong side of the window. "It's not the nicest day for it, but then it's not a nice day for much of anything."

An hour later, Caroline and Chrissy were scurrying down Broadway in the Village, sharing one inadequate umbrella. "Here, let's try this place!" Chrissy hollered above the pounding of the rain. The store didn't look especially appealing, but it was an excuse to get out of the downpour.

They left the umbrella inside the door and made their way among the cramped racks of used clothing. Caroline was the first to discover a bunch of what looked like fifties prom dresses. "I don't know," she said, frowning doubtfully. "I mean, we don't want to look like extras in the *Back to the Future* prom scene."

"Why not?" Chrissy argued, eyeing the dresses more favorably. "I think they're pretty cute."

Caroline took Chrissy's arm and dragged her to the door. "Cute is not what we're after," she instructed firmly. "Let's keep looking."

Another block down the street they found an even smaller and more crowded boutique, but

Caroline immediately judged the clothing to be of a better quality. She and Chrissy each picked out a few gowns and then ducked into a tiny dressing room together.

Chrissy struck gold with the first thing she slipped on, a midnight-blue satin strapless dress. Caroline stepped back as best she could in the cramped quarters to get a better look at her cousin. She shook her head admiringly. "Chrissy, you look smashing! Just like a movie queen— Marilyn Monroe or Rita Hayworth or something."

Chrissy pivoted slowly in front of the mirror, uncertain. The close-fitting dress flattered her curvy figure and the color was perfect, but wearing it she almost didn't recognize herself and that made her a little uncomfortable. "I don't know," Chrissy said to Caroline. "It doesn't have any straps. What if it falls down? And the skirt is so narrow. How will I walk? I don't know," she repeated. "I just don't look like *me*."

"But that's okay! You look better than you."

"Thanks a bunch," Chrissy said wryly.

"You know what I mean," Caroline said quickly, hurrying to redeem herself. "The dress looks absolutely beautiful on you. I'll be lucky if I find something half as becoming."

"Well . . ." Chrissy twirled again, admiring herself. The dress *was* beautiful, more daring and glamorous than anything she'd ever owned. She smiled at her reflection. "I think I will buy it!" she announced.

"Good. Now we just have to find something for me!"

Caroline tried on three dresses, but none of them was quite right, so after Chrissy made her purchase and saw the blue dress carefully bundled up in a watertight plastic bag, they proceeded down Broadway to several more of the popular boutiques. As Caroline tried on more and more dresses, Chrissy could see that she was becoming increasingly frustrated at not having found the ideal outfit for the cocktail party. Chrissy tried to help as much as she could, picking out dresses that she thought would suit her cousin's sophisticated style, and giving Caroline her honest opinion when something didn't. In a way she felt guilty for having found her dress first, when it was really Caroline's cocktail party.

Finally, as Caroline was in yet another dressing room, wriggling out of yet another unsuitable dress, Chrissy found the perfect outfit for her. It was a teal-green taffeta dress with a long, flounced skirt, and someone had just hung it on the dressing-room door next to Caroline's. *I guess someone tried it on and didn't like it,* she thought.

"Hey, Cara, try this one," she called, passing the dress carefully over the door to her cousin.

A moment later, Caroline swung open the dressing room door. She looked spectacular in the taffeta dress, even better than Chrissy had imagined.

"Absolutely stunning," Chrissy breathed. "Cara, you look—"

"Hey, that's it! That's my dress," a girl shrieked from across the shop. She stomped over to Caroline in her high heels, carrying several other dresses in her arms. "That's the dress I want," the girl declared. "I just hung it up on the door there so I could try these on."

Chrissy could see that Caroline was ready to give up her dress without a fight. *Well, I won't have it!* she thought. *Cara looks so terrific in that green dress, she's just got to wear it to the cocktail party.*

Chrissy studied the opposition. The girl was about her own age, but wore twice as much makeup and was weighed down by lots of gold jewelry. "Isn't there another taffeta dress on the rack?" she asked.

"Not like that one," the girl said stubbornly.

"I'll go change," Caroline said, heading back into the dressing room.

That was it. Chrissy had to do something to save the dress. She glanced down, noticing a horrible magenta-colored gown in the pile that the girl was holding. It would clash just right with the girl's dyed red hair. "Can I see that dress a minute?" she asked. Impatiently, the girl held up the dress. "My, that is lovely," Chrissy declared. "And you know, the color is much nicer than that ugly green my cousin picked out."

"Do you think so?" the girl said, a smile almost making its way across her face at the compliment.

"Oh yes," Chrissy went on. "And it really

brings out the extraordinary highlights in your hair."

The girl's eyes lit up. "Really?"

"Oh yes." Chrissy nodded emphatically. "If I were you, I'd buy that one instead of the green one."

"Thanks, I think I'll do that," the girl said, already heading toward the cash register.

Chrissy watched with a smile of satisfaction, and she was still grinning mischievously when Caroline came out of the dressing room.

"Where'd that girl go? I have her dress," Caroline said, sadly holding out the taffeta gown.

"It's your dress now," Chrissy told her.

Caroline gave her cousin a strange look. "What do you mean?"

"Let's just say that New Yorkers aren't as tough as they seem," Chrissy replied mysteriously. "Now, let's go find some accessories to match our new gowns."

Chapter 12

On Monday, Caroline and Chrissy both left work an hour early to hurry home to the loft and change for the U.N. cocktail party. As the girls asked the taxi driver to take them to the Plaza Hotel on Central Park South, they felt very important and privileged. The cocktail party was sure to be an elegant affair, for the Plaza was one of the classiest places in all of New York City. Chrissy was so excited, the only thing that prevented her from galloping through the lobby of the hotel were her high heels and tight skirt. As they entered an elevator—the fancy old-fashioned kind with an attendant—Caroline had to concentrate on keeping her nervousness under the surface. It was an honor to be invited to the party, and she wanted to make a good impression. She didn't want Juliet to regret including her and Chrissy on the guest list.

The cocktail party was in full swing when the cousins entered. "This place is huge!" Chrissy whispered to Caroline, gazing around her with wide eyes. To Chrissy, the room appeared as big as a cornfield.

"From what I hear, the Grand Ballroom is at least twice as big as this," Caroline whispered back.

The room reserved for the diplomatic function was beautiful, ornately decorated with rich velvet curtains and glimmering chandeliers. And the people—Caroline caught her breath. She'd been to lots of fancy parties with her parents in San Francisco, but certainly nothing like this! The cocktail party was more like a scene from a fairy tale than real life. Most of the men wore black tie although the girls glimpsed a few in colorful robes and turbans. But it was the women who were most stunning. Walking through the gathering was like walking through the pages of a *very* high-fashion magazine. The dresses were exquisite; there were satins and silks, gowns glittering with beads and sequins, and even one gown studded with gems. Caroline was glad now that Chrissy had gone to so much trouble to get her dress. The rustling of the taffeta seemed to give her a boost of confidence which she badly needed.

Chrissy was tagging along behind Caroline, trying not to gape. It was hard; she'd never seen such exquisitely dressed, important-looking peo-

ple in the flesh before. She knew they weren't all
ambassadors, though. In fact, some of the guys
there didn't look much older than her and
Caroline.

"There's Juliet," Caroline said, recognizing her
boss from across the room. "Let's go say hi." As
the two girls wove through the crush Caroline
suddenly recognized one of Juliet's companions
from pictures she'd seen in magazines. She
stopped in her tracks. "Chrissy!" she hissed under
her breath. "Juliet's talking to Prince Albert of
Monaco!"

Chrissy peered ahead over Caroline's shoulder.
The prince was nice-looking, but nothing spectacular in her opinion; not what she'd expected
from her first prince. "Oh, wow," Chrissy said
simply, in an appropriately awed tone.

Caroline watched for a moment as Juliet chatted with the prince. *Should Chrissy and I wait
before approaching Juliet*? she wondered. But
then her boss spotted her and beckoned her
over.

The group was speaking in French, and while
Juliet made the introductions, Caroline breathed
a secret sigh of relief that her conversational
French was as good as her written French.

Chrissy, meanwhile, was completely at sea.
She'd taken French at Maxwell High, but had
never gotten much beyond the "*Je m'appelle
Chrissy*" stage. Juliet, the prince, and the other
dignitaries were tossing around rapid-fire
phrases in what might as well have been a mar-

tian dialect. Chrissy thought Caroline looked distinctly humorous in the way she glanced raptly from one face to another, back and forth, as if she were watching a ping-pong match. "*Oui,*" Caroline would say after every second remark, nodding sagely.

Since Chrissy couldn't understand the conversation, she took the opportunity to study the elegant Prince Albert. Now he looked her way in time to catch her staring. "Excuse me," he said in English, "but have we been rude? You don't speak French?"

"Nope," Chrissy admitted brightly.

Caroline cringed.

"We were talking about the international currency problem," Prince Albert informed her. He paused as if to give Chrissy a chance to jump right in with an opinion of her own.

"The international currency problem. Hmm." Chrissy didn't see Caroline motion at her to keep her mouth closed. "Oh, I know what you mean!" she exclaimed, her eyes sparkling as if a light bulb had just gone off in her head. "It's a real pain the way different countries all have a different kind of money. Caroline was telling me once how hard it is to keep track of what's worth what. Like if you're shopping in Rome and you see a scarf you like and the price is so many Italian lire, what does that equal in American dollars?"

Caroline cleared her throat loudly and gave Chrissy another shut-up-immediately look. "We were speaking more in terms of the instability of the international money market," she told Chrissy quickly. "The relative value of some currencies keeps dwindling while others increase. It's pretty complex."

"Oh." Chrissy was silent for a minute, and a relieved Caroline turned back to Juliet, the prince, and the others and went on chatting about francs and lire and deutsche marks. During the next lull in the conversation, however, Chrissy piped up again. "How's your sister Stephanie, Prince Albert?" she asked, thinking he might enjoy talking about his family as a change of pace. "Is she still dating that—"

Chrissy was cut off mid-question when Caroline stepped sharply on her foot. "Oh, Chrissy. Those hors d'oeuvres look good." Caroline gestured vaguely. "Would you get me one?"

"Sure," Chrissy said amiably. As she turned her back on the prince, Chrissy quickly stuck her tongue out at Caroline. "You're just trying to shut me up," she accused her cousin in a whisper.

"Well, someone's got to shut you up before you make a fool of yourself in front of the prince!"

Chrissy shrugged good-naturedly. She turned her attention to waiters who looked to Chrissy like guilty butlers in a whodunit movie. The hors d'oeuvres were far more interesting than a boring conversation about international finance anyhow, Chrissy decided. She tried a miniature lobster tart and a cracker topped with smoked salmon and caviar. Then she had two melon balls wrapped in prosciutto on toothpicks, and three

cheese-and-asparagus puffs. Caroline, meanwhile, had taken the cracker Chrissy handed her
but she didn't eat it, instead holding it on a gilt-
edged cocktail napkin.

After five more minutes of chat, Prince Albert
graciously inclined his head to Juliet, Caroline,
and Chrissy and turned to greet some of the other
guests. Juliet also drifted off and Caroline and
Chrissy were left alone again.

Caroline had stars in her eyes. "I met Prince
Albert of Monaco," she said with a rapturous
sigh. "I actually *spoke* with him! In French!"

Chrissy snatched the cracker Caroline was still
holding and popped it into her own mouth."He
was okay. But have you tried these hors
d'oeuvres?" she asked, equally rapturous.
"They're amazing. Not your usual Swedish
meatballs!"

Caroline looked worriedly at Chrissy. "Don't
eat too much," she counseled her cousin in a
stern tone. "We want to look sophisticated, not
like starving street people who haven't had a
meal in days."

"Well, I'm full now anyway," Chrissy confessed. "So, who do we get to meet next?"

"Juliet just said to mingle and introduce ourselves to whoever we like," Caroline answered.
"It looks like there are pretty many young people
here. You know, like diplomatic attachés and
stuff."

"Attachés?" Chrissy wrinkled her forehead,
confused. "You mean briefcases?"

Caroline rolled her eyes. "Diplomatic attachés are like assistant diplomats," she explained patiently. "Junior staff members."

The two girls were standing along the wall, scanning the crowd to determine which direction to head in next when they were approached by two young men, looking very distinguished in crisp dinner jackets. A waiter with a tray of champagne was passing by, and each of the young men took two glasses.

The taller of the two held out a glass to Chrissy while his companion did the same to Caroline. "I am Raoul Deneuve, and this is Jean-Paul Briset," he said in slightly accented but very good English. "We are with the French delegation, at the United Nations. I hope you will join us for a cocktail."

The cousins took the offered glasses, exchanging surprised and excited glances. Raoul and Jean-Paul were both strikingly handsome, in a dark, intriguing sort of way. In Chrissy's opinion, they were a decided improvement over the rather pale prince. But even though she was ordinarily chatty and gregarious, Raoul Deneuve's stately speech left Chrissy off guard.

Caroline regained her composure first and actually managed to speak. "Of course. Thank you," she said in her coolest, most dignified manner. "I'm Caroline Kirby and this is my cousin, Christina Madden. I work at the U.N., too. I'm a high—*college* student, participating in a summer internship with the chief French translator."

Chrissy resisted a strong temptation to giggle at Caroline's half lie about being a college student. After all, wasn't Caroline always telling her not to pretend to be somebody she wasn't? Instead, she just smiled brightly, adding, "I'm an intern, too. With a magazine."

Jean-Paul and Raoul were observing Caroline and Chrissy with openly appreciative eyes. "We knew two such beautiful blond women must be Americans," Jean-Paul said now in a low, suave voice.

Chrissy darted an amused glance at Caroline. *Is this guy for real?* she wondered. But Caroline simply accepted the compliment with a gracious nod.

"And you must be native New Yorkers as well," Raoul guessed, his admiring tone making this observation another compliment.

"No, actually, I'm—we're from California," Caroline informed him. "San Francisco. We're probably more foreign to New York City than you are!"

"Hmm. In that case. . . ." Raoul glanced at his watch, which Caroline immediately judged to be a Rolex, or at least a very good imitation of one. Then he scanned the crowd, which had thinned somewhat since the girls had arrived an hour earlier. "How would you like to spend the evening with us? We could tour the city, have dinner, perhaps hear some music."

Caroline suddenly looked shy, but Chrissy had regained her voice. "We'd love to!" she accepted eagerly, fluttering her eyelashes at Raoul.

"Wonderful," Jean-Paul declared. "I will ask the porter to call our limousine. Raoul, will you attend the ladies?"

Chrissy's eyelash fluttering had worked; Raoul looked captivated. "With pleasure," he said in emphatic response to Jean-Paul's suggestion.

As Raoul took their half-empty glasses and turned to give them to a waiter, Chrissy faced Caroline quickly. "A limousine!" she whispered. "Can you believe it?"

"I know," Caroline replied, her eyes shining with excitement.

Raoul turned back to them and, offering an arm to each, said, "Shall we?"

The three strolled at a leisurely pace to the door. Caroline was conscious of the occasional eye turned their way and hoped she didn't look as awkward as she felt. Chrissy felt like royalty herself, exiting the cocktail party on the arm of a dashing Frenchman who was at least three times as handsome as some of the princes in the room.

In front of the Plaza, Jean-Paul was standing next to a long, white limousine that was pulled up to the curb. As Raoul, Chrissy, and Caroline approached, the driver hopped out to open the doors for them.

Caroline found herself in the middle seat with Jean-Paul while Chrissy and Raoul took the rear. She settled back against the leather seat cushions, turning slightly to wink at Chrissy. Chrissy missed the wink, however; her own eyes were glued to the TV set and the mini-bar, next to which stood a bucket with a bottle of champagne chilling on ice.

Jean-Paul leaned forward to speak quietly to the driver. Then he turned to the girls. "I've instructed Thomas to take us on a brief tour of the city," he said with a somewhat pompous air. "Is there any spot in particular you would desire to see?"

"Oh, we're happy to go wherever you'd like to take us," Chrissy said agreeably.

Jean-Paul mumbled again to the driver and the limousine shot off onto the street. The tour was a relatively brief one but Chrissy and Caroline knew they'd remember it for a long time. The limo moved smoothly through the traffic, its engine purring powerfully as it carried them through Central Park, which in the dusky glow of twilight looked like an enchanted forest. As they headed back down the Upper West Side toward Midtown, the distinctive tops of the Chrysler and the Empire State buildings and other skyscrapers stood out in bright relief against the darkening sky.

Raoul gripped the bottle of champagne and popped the cork. "Another glass, ladies?"

Chrissy and Caroline exchanged glances. "Um, maybe something a little lighter," Caroline said in what she hoped came across as a refined and delicate manner.

Raoul exhibited an ice-cold bottle of Perrier for her approval and when she nodded, he filled two cut-glass tumblers, topping each with a twist of lime. Then he raised his glass of champagne. "What is it they say in America? Cheers!"

"Cheers!" Jean-Paul, Caroline, and Chrissy echoed. Caroline couldn't help thinking back to the toast she'd shared with Chrissy and Rachel the night they went to the Limelight a few weeks ago. They'd hoped to meet Mr. Perfect and his best friend and they *had* met Travis and Kirk. Still, as nice and cute as Travis was, he didn't quite fit the "Mr. Perfect" bill. But Jean-Paul and Raoul were real-life Prince Charmings—sophisticated European men—just as Caroline had fantasized about meeting at the U.N.! It was really a dream come true.

The limousine had stopped at a light. Chrissy sipped her Perrier as she looked out the window, lost in a reverie of her own. It gave her a thrill to think that she could see the people waiting on the corner to cross the street but they couldn't see her through the one-way glass. She felt exotic and mysterious.

The limousine continued past Midtown, and through Greenwich Village and SoHo. "Where are we heading next?" Caroline asked Jean-Paul.

"We thought we would stop off for a bite to eat," he explained, "at a restaurant Raoul and I hope you will enjoy."

Chrissy groaned silently. After all the rich hors d'oeuvres she'd consumed at the cocktail party, she wasn't sure she could manage even just a bite. But when the limousine rolled to a stop in front of one of the World Trade Center Towers, she forgot her lack of appetite.

"You don't mind Windows on the World, do you?" Raoul asked, putting a hand on Chrissy's bare arm as he spoke.

"Oh no," Chrissy assured him nonchalantly, acting as if she and Caroline ate at the world-famous restaurant every night. "It's fine with me!"

Inside the tower, a short but terrifying elevator ride rocketed them up to the 102d floor in only a matter of seconds. Caroline turned a little pale and Chrissy felt as if she'd left her stomach behind in the lobby. But the view from the top was well worth the ride. From the windows on each side, a spectacular panorama opened out. Raoul and Jean-Paul walked Chrissy and Caroline around to enjoy the view before requesting a table. "The best table available, *s'il vous plaît*," Jean-Paul told the maitre d' in the voice of someone who was used to getting what he asked for.

The maitre d' obviously regarded the diplomatic attachés with deference, because the four were conducted to an excellent table near the window. From their seats, Chrissy and Caroline could look down on the entire island of Manhattan, spread out far below them like a scaled-down model with toy buildings and trees. The cars and buses were as small as ants and the people on the sidewalks even more minuscule. It was truly magical.

"This is wonderful," Caroline breathed, for a

moment unable to preserve her air of sophistication and experience.

"Awesome!" Chrissy agreed enthusiastically.

A grandfatherly waiter handed them their menus and announced the specials of the day. Chrissy looked at Caroline to follow her lead. She knew the food here must be incredibly expensive—she and Caroline could probably eat for a month for the cost of one meal—but she couldn't find any prices on her menu.

Raoul must have sensed her discomfort. "Order anything you like," he said expansively. He touched Chrissy's arm again. "It's our treat."

"In that case. . . ." Chrissy scanned the menu and then looked up at the waiter with a wide smile. "I'll start with the pâté. Then I'd like the shrimp and mandarin orange salad and, let's see . . . the veal Oscar. And I guess I can order my dessert later!"

Caroline also chose an appetizer and an entrée, then she pushed her chair back. "Excuse me," she said to the men, catching Chrissy's eye. "I'm going to the ladies' room."

"Me, too," Chrissy announced. "Be right back!"

The cousins strolled across the plush carpeting, aware of Raoul's and Jean-Paul's eyes on their backs. Once they were out of sight, however, and securely inside the rest room, alone except for the attendant, they burst out laughing.

"I can't believe we're here!" Caroline gasped. "Aren't Raoul and Jean-Paul handsome?"

"They're hot," Chrissy conceded, wiping the

tears of laughter from her eyes and then checking the mirror to see if her mascara had
smudged. "But are they putting on an act?
They're so gallant, it's almost too much."

"That's just the way the French treat women,"
Caroline explained knowledgeably. "They think
all women are goddesses. We might as well enjoy
it!"

"Oh, I am, I am!" Chrissy patted her stomach.
"But if I don't watch it, I'm going to pop out of this
dress. I'm not even hungry, but I felt obligated to
order every other item on the menu. I mean, I
don't know when I'll have another chance like
this!"

The meal seemed to pass quickly even though
they lingered over dinner for two hours. The
food was fantastic and Raoul and Jean-Paul
charmed Chrissy and Caroline with stories about
their experiences as diplomatic attachés and
about their homes in France. When the men suggested going on to a jazz club they frequented,
the girls eagerly agreed.

Tucked away in an obscure corner of
Greenwich Village, the club was nothing to look
at from the street, but inside it had an under-
stated elegance, and the clientele had the same
air. Caroline recognized the name of the band as
one her father, as a music critic, especially
admired.

At midnight, a second band was scheduled to
play but the four had heard enough. They
strolled down the sidewalk for a few minutes

enjoying the cool night air and then Raoul summoned the waiting limousine.

Caroline gave the driver their address and in a few minutes they had reached the loft. She looked at Chrissy and sighed, hating to see their fairy-tale evening come to an end.

Chrissy had something else in mind, though. As the limousine rolled to a stop she shocked Caroline by suddenly blurting out, "Hey, how would you guys like to come up for a drink?"

Before Caroline could protest, the men had accepted Chrissy's invitation. Raoul and Jean-Paul paused to speak with the driver while Chrissy unlocked the front door and turned the key for the elevator. "What do you mean, a drink?" Caroline asked her cousin in a sharp whisper.

"Roy Fisher has a fully stocked bar," Chrissy reminded her mischievously. "Don't tell me you want to say good-bye to that gorgeous Jean-Paul yet. I sure don't want to say goodnight to Raoul!"

Raoul and Jean-Paul praised the loft's decor and Mr. Fisher's art collection. "And now how about that drink," Raoul said to Chrissy as he made himself comfortable on one of the low, cushiony sofas. "Can you manage a martini?"

"Can I manage a martini!" Chrissy laughed lightly at Raoul, passing his query off as a joke. At the same time, she darted a desperate glance at Caroline.

Caroline did manage to toss her cousin a tip as Chrissy passed on her way to the bar. "There's a bartending guide on the top shelf, behind the seltzer!" Caroline whispered, turning on the stereo to a popular jazz station. She felt awkward with Jean-Paul and Raoul in the loft.

"Wish me luck!" Chrissy replied.

She found the guide and, keeping her back carefully turned to Raoul and Jean-Paul, began flipping rapidly through the pages. "Mai Tai, Manhattan, Margarita, Martini!" she muttered under her breath. "Gin and vermouth? That sounds easy. And what is it James Bond always says: 'Shaken, not stirred'? I can handle this!"

A few minutes later, Chrissy proudly presented Raoul and Jean-Paul with their martinis. Instead of thanking her, Raoul merely pulled her down on the couch next to him. She wasn't sure how he managed to juggle his glass—it felt as if both his hands were all over her. As soon as she pushed one off her shoulder it reappeared on her waist or her knee.

Jean-Paul had his own arm firmly around Caroline, who was looking equally trapped and uncomfortable. She kept trying to turn away, pretending that she had to get up and tune the stereo or get napkins for the drinks, but Jean-Paul seemed to have no intention of letting her go. To make matters worse, the two diplomatic attachés were still telling stories about themselves and wouldn't let the girls get a word in edgewise.

"Have I told you about the occasion when the president of France visited my family at our ancestral chateau in the Loire Valley?" Raoul asked Chrissy in a suave, pompous tone.

Chrissy started to say, "Yes, at least a dozen times!" but Raoul had already launched into the recollection. Jean-Paul, meanwhile, had drained his martini and was talking in low, romantic tones to Caroline, his mouth only half an inch from her ear.

Caroline took advantage of Jean-Paul's position to sneak a glance at her watch and then one at Chrissy. Chrissy got the hint her cousin was sending, and it was clear they had the same idea. Raoul and Jean-Paul were becoming insufferable. It was time to get rid of them.

"Oh, my, it sure is getting late," Chrissy observed, interrupting Raoul and putting a hand to her mouth to cover an exaggerated yawn. "I suppose you guys have to be at work pretty early tomorrow, like me and Caroline?"

"Oh, no," Raoul said, pulling Chrissy closer to his side. Neither he nor Jean-Paul made any gesture towards leaving. "We can make our own hours, you know," he explained in a self-important voice.

"Oh." Chrissy shrugged helplessly in Caroline's direction. "That's nice."

Caroline racked her brain for another strategy but nothing occurred to her. When Raoul and Jean-Paul asked Chrissy to make them a second round of martinis, she really started to panic. What if they never left? Judging from the way Jean-Paul was caressing the back of her neck with his hand, he expected to be invited to stay all night.

Chrissy delivered the martinis, then remained standing several feet away from Raoul so he couldn't pull her down next to him again. She caught Caroline's desperate expression and knew it was time to take action, Chrissy Madden style. She had an idea of what would really turn off these fastidious Frenchmen.

All of a sudden, Chrissy clapped a hand to her mouth and let out a piercing shriek. Caroline jumped out of her seat at the sound. "A rat!" Chrissy hollered, leaping to her feet. She jumped onto the sofa, struggling all the while to hold onto her strapless gown. "A rat!" she repeated, louder this time.

Caroline followed Chrissy's lead and screamed also, running around the sofa in a crazy circle before jumping on top of it.

Raoul and Jean-Paul looked distinctly uncomfortable, as if they would have loved to hop on the couches, too, but their male dignity wouldn't allow them.

Now Caroline had her own inspiration. "Chrissy!" she yelled at her cousin. "Get the pistol and shoot this one the way you did the others!" Caroline pointed toward the kitchen. She was pretty sure the water pistol Chrissy had bought for her little brother was still sitting on the butcher-block counter.

Chrissy's eyes sparkled as she grasped Caroline's meaning and dashed into the kitchen.

By the time she came out brandishing a loaded pink water pistol, Raoul and Jean-Paul had hurried to the elevator, trying not to appear *too* horrified.

Raoul was fumbling with the key in the switch. Caroline stepped calmly to his side. "Here, let me," she offered sweetly, turning the key. When the elevator arrived she stepped inside for a moment to direct it down to the first floor with the other key, hopping back just before the door slid shut. "Thanks for a great evening, guys!" she called as Raoul and Jean-Paul disappeared from view.

"Yeah, thanks!" Chrissy echoed, waving her watergun cheerfully.

"*Mon dieu*, so much for our taste of the high life," Caroline observed with a giggle that faded into a sigh of relief.

"Yeah, but it was fun while it lasted, huh?" Chrissy said, grinning.

Caroline's eyelids dropped and her vision of the room blurred. For a second, she imagined herself back in the Plaza meeting Prince Albert; then she was transported in a sleek limousine to Windows on the World, sampling the finest cuisine in the city. "Yes, it was fun," she agreed wholeheartedly.

But as usual, Chrissy got the last word in. Squirting Caroline with the water pistol, she yelled, "Last one to bed is a rotten egg!"

Chapter 13

Chrissy popped out of the elevator after work on Thursday, broadcasting an announcement. "Guess what we're doing tomorrow?"

"Not horseback riding again, I hope," Caroline said in an apprehensive tone. She was standing at the kitchen counter rinsing off a bunch of grapes. "I was in agony all day. It hurts to sit down," she complained. "I'm sore in places where I didn't even know I had muscles! And I used to think ballet was strenuous."

"It's just because you're not used to it. And anyway, we're not going horseback riding," Chrissy assured her cousin. Her eyes twinkled as she thought of their ride the day before. It was their last week in New York and the cousins were cramming in all the action they could before they left for home. After work on Wednesday they had met at a riding stable near Central Park West and rented saddle horses for an hour. Chrissy had been in seventh heaven, pretending she was cantering on Posey, her mare in Iowa. Caroline, on the other hand, was a beginner and had confined herself to a stiff, bouncing trot. Chrissy would have considered Caroline's mount, Brownie, an old nag, but to Caroline the horse seemed enormous and overly frisky. She had to admit she'd had fun, though, and she'd laughed as hard as Chrissy when Brownie shied at a passing jogger, nearly tossing Caroline into the shrubbery.

"Nope, not horseback riding," Chrissy repeated. "You'll never guess in a million years, so I'll just tell you." She paused to pluck a few grapes from the bunch, making the most of the moment of suspense. "We're going to be *Heart Throb*'s fashion make-overs of the month!"

"What?" Caroline squealed, forgetting about her aching muscles and jumping up and down with excitement. "No way! You're putting me on!"

Chrissy shook her head, grinning from ear to ear. "Unh-uh, it's no put-on. They threw a surprise going-away party for me today at the office, and Stephen, the fashion editor, told me the news. I almost died! They're going to take before and after pictures of us at one of the studios at the magazine. Cara, they'll do our hair and makeup the way they do models', and we'll get to pose in the trendiest clothes! Then, in a couple of months we'll actually be on the pages of *Heart Throb*."

Caroline danced forward to give Chrissy a spontaneous hug. "I can't believe it," she exclaimed. "This is great! You and me, actually in a magazine!"

"I know. It was Sophie's idea. She's the one who told Stephen you were as photogenic as I was. Then they came up with a theme for the make-over." Chrissy grinned wickedly. "I just can't wait to send a couple of copies to Ben and Luke just to give them a taste of what they're missing these days by dating dull little old farm girls!"

Caroline smiled, amused by Chrissy's blood-thirsty plan for revenge. That would show Ben and Luke, all right. Then, all of a sudden a thought struck Caroline. It had been a while, a couple of days at least, since she'd really missed Luke. The last week or so she'd been too busy to even think about him, or to think about anything other than winding up her U.N. internship, and squeezing in all the crazy outings and shopping sprees with Chrissy that she could. Nearly all month, Luke had been right with Caroline even though he was a thousand miles away. He'd stayed on her mind no matter how hard she tried to push him out.

Now she discovered he was finally where he belonged—at a distance. Well, she still missed him. Here she was thinking about him again. But Caroline realized she missed him in a different way. She wasn't bitter, she wasn't hurt, she wasn't as lonely as she'd been a few weeks ago. She almost felt like she was ready to talk to him and be friends again. Of course it was impossible . . . wasn't it? She'd blown up at him and cut things off cold. And while it was a distinct possibility that she would bump into him at some point during the two days she spent in Danbury before she flew home, it was equally possible he'd be with Tammy Laudenschlager when she did. In that case, Caroline supposed she wasn't really ready to be friends again. It made more sense to just keep on forgetting about him, a little bit more each day.

Chrissy was oblivious to the daydreamy expression that had stolen over Caroline's face. After pausing to polish off the grapes she began chattering again. "Oh, and I almost forgot to tell you! *Heart Throb* invited me to come back to work for them next year, for the whole summer!"

Caroline snapped back to reality. "Congratulations, Chrissy. And that reminds *me*. Today Juliet asked me to consider working at the U.N. again next summer, too!"

The cousins high-fived one another. Chrissy leaned back against the counter, looking around at the loft's high-tech kitchen. "Of course we wouldn't be able to live here," she said regretfully. "Unless Roy Fisher goes on another tour!"

"Hmm. Yeah, we'd have to pay through our teeth for some tiny apartment the size of a closet," Caroline agreed.

They were silent for a moment and then

Chrissy said slowly, "I've had a lot of fun living in New York, but. . . ."

"*But*," Caroline echoed. "It's a big wonderful city. But one month might be enough for a lifetime!"

"It's just a long way from home," Chrissy said, her blue eyes thoughtful. "And even though a month ago I couldn't wait to get out of Danbury, now I'm looking forward to going back. And next summer, after a year at school in Colorado, I bet I'll be dying to be home on the farm."

"So what did you tell Sophie about working for the magazine?"

"I said thanks, I'd think about it."

Caroline smiled. "That's exactly what I said!"

"Well, there's no point in limiting ourselves, right?" Chrissy said logically. "Who knows how many other exciting offers we might get between now and next June!"

"Chrissy, is that you?" Caroline asked teasingly.

Chrissy pretended not to hear her question. "Excuse me, glamorous stranger, have you seen my plain-Jane cousin Caroline?"

"Thanks a lot!" Caroline sounded irate but she was laughing.

It was Friday evening and the crew at *Heart Throb* had agreed to stay late to do the make-overs. The cousins were in the dressing room adjacent to the studio where their make-over photos had just been shot. They both sat in front of a big mirror, ogling their reflections. Neither girl looked much like her usual self.

Chrissy's straw-straight hair had been teased into a full, fluffy mass. The heavy eye makeup made her bright blue eyes jump right out of her face. The T-shirt and jumper that she'd worn to work had been replaced by a skintight red jersey mini-dress, cinched in at the waist with a wide leather belt. In spike heels, her legs looked like they went on forever.

The fashion editor had created a somewhat softer, cooler look for Caroline, whose straight hair had been parted low on one side and swept back off her face. Underneath the boxy striped jacket, she wore a skimpy tank top made out of the same soft, flowing silk as her narrow trousers. Long earrings dangled to her shoulders, matched by a cluster of necklaces at her throat.

Chrissy and Caroline gathered up their pocketbooks and old clothes—they had been thrilled to learn that they could keep the new outfits—and after saying goodbye to the few people still hanging around the office, rode the elevator down to the lobby of the Flatiron Building.

"Talk about all dressed up and no place to go!" Caroline observed to Chrissy as they joined the end of the rush hour traffic on the sidewalk, heading in the direction of the subway station.

"Well, we'll just have to make a night of it!" Chrissy said, enjoying the occasional stares of passersby. "How about calling Travis and Kirk and meeting at the Limelight?"

"I don't know. My outfit isn't really right for dancing. I'd hate to sweat all over this silk!"

They were on the subway now, standing up in the cramped car and keeping their balance by holding onto the metal handrails. "I know," Caroline said as she was struck by a brilliant inspiration. "I'm sure Roy Fisher wouldn't mind. Let's have a party at the loft!"

Chrissy loved the idea and the moment they stepped through the door of the apartment she was on the telephone dialing everyone she'd met in New York. "No one's home," she informed Caroline in a forlorn tone as she slammed the receiver down after the fifth unsuccessful call. "I've tried Jackie and Bernard and José, and even Travis and Kirk. Not one of them answered!"

"Here, let me try." Caroline reached for the phone herself. "I'll call Rachel and the other kids I work with at the U.N."

But Caroline drew a blank, too. Chrissy pouted, disappointed. "It's our very last Friday night in New York City and nobody we know even has the decency to be home when we call!" Chrissy wailed. "I might as well change into my old overalls and T-shirt right this minute. There doesn't seem to be much point in looking like a real New Yorker if I'm just going to be hanging around with you."

"Gee, thanks," Caroline said sarcastically. "I enjoy your company, too!"

Just then the intercom buzzed. Chrissy bounced over to the wall and pushed the button on the speaker. "Who is it?" she asked curiously.

"Delivery—florist," a voice announced.

"Flowers!" Chrissy shrieked. "Come on up in the elevator!"

"Flowers?" Caroline echoed, mystified, as the elevator began to creak upward. "Who do you suppose they're for? Who do you suppose they're *from*?"

"They're probably for you," Chrissy conceded. "Maybe from Travis. Maybe he hasn't given up on you yet. Or they could be from Jean-Paul and Raoul. They want another taste of my martinis!"

"And another encounter with our rats!" Caroline added. Chrissy hooted.

The elevator had groaned to a stop. Caroline thought she heard a muffled giggle but before she could speculate about it, the door slid open.

"Surprise!" a dozen voices shouted in unison.

The elevator was packed to the ceiling with bodies, and now they all poured out, surrounding a shocked Chrissy and Caroline and showering them with hugs and kisses. Travis and Kirk, the three *Heart Throb* interns that Chrissy had just tried to call, and Rachel and the other four U.N. interns were all there, along with armfuls of surprises. Rachel had a bouquet of multicolored balloons; Travis had a bouquet of white roses; Jackie carried a grocery bag overflowing with chips and pretzels; Kirk lugged a case of soda; and Claudine held a homemade chocolate cake.

"Surprise, surprise!" Travis was still shouting. Then he took a closer look at Caroline. "Hey, excuse me. We must have the wrong loft. We were looking for a couple of laid-back California girls. You two chic New Yorkers must be waiting for your evening escorts." His eyes became teasing. "Maybe a couple of ultrasuave French diplomatic attaches?"

Caroline blushed hotly. "Who told you that story?" she demanded to know, looking accusingly at Chrissy.

Chrissy shrugged helplessly. "Guilty as charged," she confessed. "It was too good not to share!"

"And share some more!" Bernard agreed.

Caroline had to laugh. They were exactly right—she had told the story at least twenty times since Monday. "Whose idea was this anyway?" she asked.

Paco pushed Rachel forward. "Blame her," he advised Caroline. "She got us all so teary eyed at work today talking about how tragic it was going to be when you left the U.N., and how your cousin's friends at *Heart Throb* were probably equally devastated. So we thought we might as well just get together and sob!"

Rachel gave Paco a pinch. "Get together and *party*, have one last great time," she corrected him.

Chrissy had trotted over to the stereo and now music was blasting from Mr. Fisher's state-of-the-art compact disc player. The snacks and drinks were quickly distributed around the living room—there were pretzels balanced on the head of one sculpture and the cake perched on top of another. Chrissy and Bernard got the dancing started and Caroline tried, fairly successfully, not to be jealous when Travis danced first with Rachel, leaving her to be Tad's partner.

During a break in the music, Caroline and Rachel converged at Claudine's chocolate cake. "Having fun?" Rachel asked, giving Caroline a quick hug before sampling the frosting with her finger.

Caroline smiled. "I really am. This was the sweetest idea, Rachel. Really. Thanks for making Chrissy's and my last weekend so special!"

"You deserve it. We really are going to miss you." Rachel's eyes misted over with sudden tears. "Oops! There I go. Don't let Paco see me. I'll never hear the end of it!"

Caroline was sniffling herself. "Don't forget to give me your address before you leave. Then I can write from Colorado when I know my address! I really want to stay in touch."

"Me, too." Rachel finished her cake and then glanced in the direction of the stereo, where Chrissy and Travis were flipping through Mr. Fisher's CD collection. "Caroline, I hope you didn't mind me dancing with Travis," she said.

"Not at all," Caroline assured her sincerely. "There's not anything between us but friendship at this point."

"He's a great guy," Rachel observed thoughtfully. "Your guy from Iowa must really be wonderful if Travis came in second place to him!"

"Yeah, he is—*was* wonderful," Caroline said softly. Then she jumped to her feet, refusing to let thoughts of Luke intrude on tonight. "C'mon. First one across the room gets to dance with Travis next!"

The party ran late. Between eating, drinking, dancing, talking, and Chrissy's reenactment of the "Rat!" scene with Raoul and Jean-Paul, the time flew by. It was two o'clock in the morning before anyone knew it.

The good-byes were both funny and sad. Rachel and Caroline sniffled some more while Chrissy and the *Heart Throb* gang traded a few final jokes and reminiscences from the past month. Kirk and Travis were the last to leave. Kirk enveloped Chrissy in a friendly bear hug while Travis gave Caroline a gentle kiss on the cheek.

"I won't forget you," he promised. "If you're ever in New York again . . ."

"It was fun," Caroline agreed. Her voice trembled slightly. "'Bye, Travis."

The elevator door closed and Travis and Kirk were gone.

Before going to bed, Chrissy and Caroline trailed tiredly around the loft, collecting empty cups and sweeping up potato chip crumbs. The last cup disposed of, Chrissy collapsed on her favorite sofa. "Fun night, huh?" she asked Caroline.

"You bet." Caroline made a funny face, half-smile and half-yawn. "Did you notice who seemed to be hitting it off tonight? Travis and Rachel!"

"You don't say!" Chrissy ran her hands through her still-fluffy hair. "That's a pretty funny coincidence."

"Well, now that I think about it, they're perfect for each other," Caroline commented. "Maybe I'll take credit for matching them up!"

"You're not sorry you didn't match yourself up with Travis?" Chrissy asked.

"No, not at all," Caroline said firmly. "I'm happy with the way things worked out. I made some close friends and had a lot of fun. I have memories that'll last forever. This has really been a perfect month."

"Same here," Chrissy agreed wholeheartedly. "You know, I was really sad to say goodbye to everyone."

The girls turned out the living-room lights, then headed together to the bedroom to undress and carefully hang up their make-over outfits. Yawning, Caroline felt herself gravitating toward her bed like steel to a magnet.

Chrissy wanted to talk some more, but when Caroline responded by snoring, she abandoned the attempt. Snuggling under the covers, Chrissy closed her eyes. *A perfect month . . .*

Chapter 14

Saturday was clear and breezy, as if the city wanted Chrissy and Caroline to remember it at its best. Unfortunately, the girls had to spend half the day packing. They had a very early flight out of Newark the next morning.

Chrissy had been struggling with her enormous, well-worn suitcase for fifteen minutes but now she gave up. It absolutely refused to shut.

"Darn old thing!" Chrissy panted, kicking it irritably.

"Want me to sit on it while you try to snap it closed?" Caroline offered, looking up from the clothes she was folding.

"That'd do a lot of good," Chrissy said grumpily. "You're such a featherweight. It would take ten of you to make a dent in this baby!"

"Well, face it." Caroline put her hands on her hips and surveyed the overflowing contents of Chrissy's suitcase. "You have at least twice as much stuff as you did when you got here—all your new clothes, and the presents for your family. What did you expect?"

"You're right, Cara," Chrissy admitted with a sigh. She bent over to give the suitcase a pat, as if to make up for the kick. Then she looked hopefully at her cousin. "I don't suppose you'll have any extra room in *your* bag?"

"You supposed right," Caroline said briskly, placing a neat stack of cotton sweaters in her own suitcase. "Sorry, no space here!"

Chrissy flung up her hands in defeat. Then she sat down on the floor to put on her sneakers. "I know what I'll do. I'm going to run out to the Gap and buy one of those big canvas shoulderbags. That should hold everything I can't fit in the suitcase. A bag like that'll probably come in handy at college anyway."

"Pick up something for lunch, will you?" Caroline asked. They had cleaned out the refrigerator and there wasn't much to eat. "I thought I could scrape by with just some fruit, but all this packing has made me hungry!"

"Sure thing. See you in a bit!" Chrissy waved and then disappeared into the living room. A few seconds later, Caroline heard the creaking of the elevator. Another minute or so passed and then, to her surprise, she heard the elevator swishing open again. Chrissy reappeared, sticking her head around the door to the bedroom, an odd expression on her face.

"Here's the mail," she said, sounding excited for some reason. "I checked the box and then, I, um, just thought I'd bring it up before I went out. 'Bye! I'll be back soon."

Chrissy dashed off again and Caroline idly picked up the stack of mail to flip through it. Most of it was addressed to Roy Fisher, as usual. Then her heart stopped with a jolt. *Caroline Kirby*, the last envelope in the pile read. Caroline would know that handwriting anywhere, even if the return address didn't confirm her guess. It was a letter from Luke!

She sat down abruptly on the bed, stunned. A letter from Luke, after all these weeks! Caroline's hands shook as she brought the letter closer to her face, peering at it as if she could read the contents through the envelope. What would it say? In an instant, she imagined the worst. Luke was writing to tell her that he and Tammy were getting married, so his breakup with Caroline was really and truly official.

Caroline felt cold. All of a sudden she didn't want to open the letter. But the suspense was too painful. With a swift gesture, she ripped the envelope open and pulled out the sheet of lined notebook paper, crowded with writing in small, endearingly sloppy print. She took a deep, shaky breath and began reading.

Dear Caroline,

You're probably surprised to hear from me. Well, I got the address from Mrs. Madden and then it was just a question of screwing up my nerve to actually write!

I bet with all the people you've been meeting in New York City you've already forgotten about me, but I had to take the chance that maybe you still think about me sometimes. Because I think about you—a lot. I've been really bummed about our last phone call. I hated to think the last time we ever talked to each other we'd had a fight. And I know it was all my fault, so I'd like to apologize. I was wrong to see another girl behind your back. What can I say—I missed you, and Tammy's company was better than moping around the pigpens by myself!

But that's not why I'm writing. I'm writing because I can't stand the thought that I might never see you again. I don't want to break up—I never did. I'm sorry for everything that's happened and I want to make it up to you. I really think we can work things out if we try. Fort Collins isn't that far away from Colorado University.

I love you, Caroline. Please call me when you get this letter if you still love me. It would make me so happy to hear your voice again! If you don't call, well, I'll know what that means. I miss you.

Love, Luke.

Caroline read the letter twice and then she folded it carefully and put it back in the envelope. She could feel the heat in her face and she knew she was smiling. Luke was sorry! He loved her and wanted to get back together!

Call me if you still love me. . . . Fort Collins isn't that far away from Colorado University. . . . Caroline walked slowly into the living room and then stopped by the phone, biting her lip. It would be easy—all she had to do was pick up the receiver and dial the numbers. So how come her arm was frozen at her side and wouldn't move?

She sat down on the sofa and took another deep breath, amazed at how nervous she was. "Hey, you're in control," Caroline said out loud. She paused, feeling her heart pounding in her chest, then went on with her pep talk. "He's the one asking forgiveness. It's yours to give. So, *call!*"

Grabbing the phone, Caroline dialed Luke's number as fast as she could, before she had a chance to chicken out. She was half hoping for a busy signal so she'd have a little more time to consider what she was doing, but the line was clear and the phone began ringing.

Caroline held her breath. One ring . . . two rings . . . three rings . . . "Hello?"

It was Luke's deep voice. All of a sudden tears of longing sprang into Caroline's eyes. "Hi, Luke?" she said, her tone hesitant.

"Caroline!" he exclaimed hoarsely. "Is that you?"

"Of course," she replied, trying to keep her manner light. "Who else would get your letter and run to the phone to call you ten seconds later?"

"I can't believe it. I just can't believe it," he said, his voice cracking slightly. "It's really you!"

"Yeah," Caroline said softly. "It's really me."

There was an awkward silence. Caroline didn't know what she was supposed to say next. Then Luke spoke. "So . . . You got my letter?" he said.

Caroline laughed. "Yes, I got your letter. I'm not a mind reader! Thanks—thanks for writing. Your letter . . . well, it really made me happy. I wanted to let you know that I'm as sorry as you are. About what happened last time we talked, I mean."

"I've gone over that conversation so many times in my mind," Luke said. "I kept wishing I hadn't let you go so easily."

"Well, I was mad," Caroline reminded him. "Nothing you could have said would have made me feel any better about you and—and that awful Tammy person."

"You had every right to be mad," Luke admitted. Caroline could almost see his sheepish grin. "But nothing happened, Cara, I promise. And anyway, she's seeing some other guy now."

"Oh, so that's why you wrote to me?" Caroline said. She tried to sound casual, but suddenly she felt fearful again. "Nothing better to do with your time?"

"Now, Cara, that's not what I meant at all and

you know it," Luke said firmly and Caroline let out a sigh of relief. "You've gotta believe me— you're the only person I've been thinking about this whole darn summer."

"Same here," Caroline confessed softly.

"You mean you haven't met a guy in New York?" Now Luke sounded very relieved.

"Oh, I met some guys," Caroline said, thinking of Travis and Jean-Paul. "But nothing happened, Luke, I promise," she added, using Luke's own expression.

Luke laughed heartily, the sound a little scratchy over the long-distance line. "All right, we're even. Does that mean we can start over?"

"I want to," Caroline said, her whole heart in her words. "But Luke, it was so hard trying to keep a long-distance relationship going. I want to start over, I really do. But I just don't know if it'll work. I'll be at Colorado University and you'll be at Fort Collins. I know that's a lot closer than California and Iowa, but still. Some other Tammy-type will come along. . . ." Caroline's voice trailed off unhappily.

"You're still mad at me about that, too, huh?" Luke guessed.

"A little," Caroline admitted. "Things could have been perfect for us, Luke, if you'd only decided to go to Colorado University like we planned."

"Perfect for *you*, maybe." Luke was silent for a moment. "Colorado University's the right place for you, Caroline, and I'm happy for you. But it wasn't what I was looking for. You know me—you know what I want to do. I love flying. If I'd gone to Colorado University I'd just have been following you. It would have been a big mistake." Caroline sniffled. "Hey, no more sad sounds. I didn't say our relationship was a big mistake, did I?"

"No." Caroline wiped her nose on the sleeve of the Columbia sweat shirt Kirk and Travis had given her for a going-away present.

"You're the best thing that's ever happened to me," Luke assured her, his voice strong and honest. "I still want to be part of your life, and I want you to be part of mine. So," he continued hopefully, "if you wanted we could visit each other. You could road-trip to Fort Collins and I could come see you in Boulder. It wouldn't be that far, just a couple of hours; maybe not even."

Luke didn't have to wait long for Caroline's answer. She knew that he was right, about so many things. She'd been selfish to expect him to go to Colorado University just so they could be together. She'd faulted him for not being flexible enough when in fact she was the stubborn one. "I'd like that," she said sincerely. "I'd really like that."

Instead of sounding overjoyed, however, now Luke sighed somewhat impatiently. "If only we didn't have to wait that long to see each other again," he said. "By the time we both get settled in at school, it'll be the end of September, maybe even October!"

Caroline smiled again. Did she ever have a surprise for Luke! "Oh, didn't I mention it?" she said casually. "Guess where I'll be tomorrow afternoon? Danbury, Iowa!"

The line crackled loudly as Luke yelled "Yahoo!" on the other end.

"I'll only be there for two days," Caroline cautioned him. "It's just a stopover on my way home to San Francisco."

"But I'll get to see you," Luke said, unbelieving. "Somebody's really been listening to my prayers. There's nothing I want more right now than just a few minutes with you, just to see your face while I talk to you!"

"Me, too," Caroline said, her own heart racing at the prospect. "Well . . . I should go. This is Roy Fisher's phone bill, after all."

"Okay. I'll call you tomorrow night at the Maddens'." Luke paused. "And, Cara? Thanks for giving me—us—another chance. I love you. I can't wait to see you."

Caroline swallowed. She hadn't said the words in a long time and her throat was a little rusty. "I love you, too, Luke," she managed to croak out. "I can't wait to see you, either."

"G'bye, Caroline."

"'Bye, Luke."

Caroline hung up the phone and then sank back limply on the couch, feeling as if all her bones had melted. It was like being disembodied, and she had a feeling that if she stood up right now she'd literally be able to walk on air. Luke still loved her! And she knew that no matter how mad she'd been about his seeing another girl, she'd never stopped caring about him. Tomorrow night they'd see each other; they'd have a chance to say all the things that were impossible to talk about over the phone. She was definitely glad she'd planned to visit Chrissy's family on her way back to San Francisco—*very* glad.

Caroline had put her feet up on the sofa and was singing a corny tune from *Oklahoma!* when the elevator clattered to a stop and Chrissy sprang through the door into the loft, her arms overflowing with shopping bags. "Well, what did he say? What did he say?" she demanded, dropping the bags on the floor and bouncing up and down on the sofa next to Caroline.

Caroline blushed but she couldn't help grinning. "Well . . . I think we have a date for tomorrow night in Danbury!"

"Oh, Cara!" Chrissy leaned forward to squeeze Caroline in a warm bear hug. "I'm so happy for you. I knew that idiot would see the light."

"He saw the light," Caroline agreed with a soft smile. "We both saw the light."

"Well, there's no need to cry about it," Chrissy exclaimed, noticing that Caroline's eyes were misting over with tears. "This calls for a celebration!" She jumped up and retrieved the shopping bags. "And, what a coincidence. I came home prepared for a party!"

"What?" Caroline said. "But we just had a party last night."

"I know," Chrissy replied, "but this party is just for us, and"—she pointed to the sculptures scattered around the room—"them."

Caroline looked at her cousin as if she had finally cracked, but she couldn't help grinning with admiration. What a great idea!

Out of the shopping bag came a cold bottle of Caroline's favorite peach-flavored seltzer and a bag of Gianetti's most sinful pastries. There was a package of balloons which Caroline began inflating while Chrissy hopped around the room decorating the sculptures with party hats and Groucho Marx-style glasses complete with noses and mustaches. "I think we should leave the sculptures dressed up like this, don't you? As a surprise for Mr. Fisher," Chrissy suggested, eyeing her handiwork with pleasure.

Caroline burst out laughing in the middle of blowing up a balloon. The half-filled balloon escaped and whizzed around the living room, deflating with a screech. "I just hope he has a sense of humor!" Caroline said.

Chapter 15

"It seems like just yesterday we were sitting here after our first day at our internships, doesn't it?" Chrissy said to Caroline.

The cousins had finished straightening up the loft and packing an hour before. Chrissy had transferred her surplus belongings into her new canvas shoulderbag and with Caroline's help had finally managed to close the troublesome suitcase. Caroline had reread Luke's letter three more times before placing it tenderly in her own neat but jam-packed suitcase. For dinner they'd decided to eat at their favorite restaurant in SoHo, the Orange Blossom Cafe, and they had chosen the same rickety table where they'd sat the first time.

"I know." The late-afternoon breeze ruffled

Caroline's blond bangs. She put up a hand to push them off her forehead. "I don't think a month has ever gone by so fast for me!"

"Me, neither." Chrissy shook her head. "Think of all the things that happened to us in just a month!"

"Well . . ." Caroline lifted her glass of mango juice in Chrissy's direction. "Here's to a great time in the Big Apple!"

Chrissy raised her Coke likewise. "Cheers!" she said with enthusiasm. "And I have another toast, looking in the other direction—ahead. Here's to four great years at Colorado University!"

As Caroline sipped at her mango juice, a chill ran down her spine that wasn't just a result of the cool breeze on her bare arms. In another month she and Chrissy would be busy packing again, this time for *college*. And they wouldn't just be visiting in Boulder; they'd be living there. Like Chrissy said, for four whole years. It was an exciting, scary thought.

Chrissy was on the same wavelength. "I'm pretty glad we only came to New York for a month," she said, snapping a breadstick thoughtfully in two. "September's coming up fast enough. It'll be sort of nice to have some time at home, to hang around with my family and get ready for college."

"I was just thinking the same thing," Caroline confessed. "Coming out here, I missed a whole month with everyone at home. Maria, Tracy, Justine—everybody'll be heading off in different directions so soon. I'm sure we'll keep in touch, but it won't ever be like it was in high school. It'll be great to have all of August to go to the beach and stuff. And do things with my parents—I won't be able to afford to take myself to the opera or the symphony when I'm a poor student in Boulder!"

Chrissy sighed. "Yep, just one more month to fatten myself up on my mom's fantastic cooking before I face the institutional food at the university."

Caroline felt full just thinking about the kind of meals that were served at the Maddens' house. "I'm sure you'll waste away," she said dryly. "Anyway, that's why pizza was invented."

Just then, the waiter arrived with their dinners, and the girls stopped talking in order to dig in.

"I'm stuffed," Chrissy admitted an hour later after devouring a triple fudge torte for dessert. They paid their check and headed off down the sidewalk. "I'm glad we have a long walk home. I need to work some of those calories off."

"Then you'd better walk up to Central Park and back," Caroline teased.

They strolled slowly west, in the direction of the loft. The sun had just set and the sky ahead of them was shot through with orange and purple, fading to pale green and blue. The breeze that whispered through the leaves of the little trees planted along the sidewalk carried with it all the various city smells they'd become familiar with. The cafes, the movie theaters, the unusual shops, the unusual people; all of it had been so foreign at first, but now Chrissy and Caroline could walk around with confidence. It had really been a remarkable month. As they rounded the corner and turned onto their street, Caroline realized that this month in New York had prepared her for college in more ways than one. She'd gotten a chance to live away from home, and she'd survived pretty well, only having been homesick once or twice. She'd been exposed to a new world, met new people, and learned a new job, and she'd managed so well that she'd been invited to work at the U.N. again next summer.

Yes, it had been fun to be independent, seek new experiences and adventures. One thing she had learned, though, was that all the new experiences in the world couldn't erase the memory of an old experience. But she was lucky. Her relationship with Luke wasn't going to end up as just a memory. They were starting over, as of tomorrow!

Chrissy and Caroline reached the apartment building and Chrissy fumbled in the pocket of her denim jacket for the keys. As Chrissy turned the key in the door and then pushed it open, Caroline looked back over her shoulder one last time. "Good-bye, New York," she whispered.

Here's a sneak preview of *Campus Cousins*, book number seventeen in the continuing SUGAR & SPICE series from Ivy Books:

"Are you sure you want to do this?" Caroline's roommate Ellis Lattimore asked her on a Sunday afternoon.

"Yes. Joining Sigma Theda will be a great way to get involved on campus." Caroline checked her appearance in the mirror for the fourth time. "Do I look all right?"

Ellis frowned as she studied Caroline. "The silk dress is perfect for the Sigmas, but you need pearls."

"I don't have any," Caroline answered despondently. Whenever she'd worn pearls in the past, Caroline had always borrowed them from her mother.

"Don't worry. You can wear mine," Ellis volunteered.

"Thanks!" said Caroline. She peered over her shoulder, checking her panty hose for any runs down the back of her legs. The Sigma Thedas were known for noticing little details.

Ellis fastened the pearls around Caroline's neck. "You look great. The Sigmas are the most socially prominent people on campus. They are going to love you!"

"I hope so." Caroline made a big deal of crossing her fingers and Ellis laughed. It was nice to have a roommate who understood. When she'd called Chrissy for the meeting place and time, her cousin had been more interested in why she wanted to join some Greek club than in finding the information for her on the list.

She still had her fingers crossed when she reached the three-block area on Aspen Street where the sorority and fraternity houses dominated both sides of the road. Caroline had to wonder which sorority was having the party at 140 Aspen. The girls talking on the porch were well dressed. In case the Sigma Thedas didn't fall in love with her, this sorority might be a good second choice.

It seemed odd to Caroline as she walked farther down Aspen that the prestigious Sigma Theda would have their house at the end of the Greek territory. When she found 124 Aspen, she carefully checked the notes she had taken during her phone call with Chrissy. Although the yard was mowed and the curtains in the front window looked crisp and white, there was a quiet atmosphere about the house that just didn't fit her idea of the Sigma Thedas. But 124 was the number on the slip of paper she pulled out of her purse.

Taking a deep breath, she climbed the steps. This was going to be one of the most important hours in her college career.

A tall, thin girl opened the front door. "Welcome. I'm Betty."

"I'm Caroline Kirby."

"Kirby?" Betty cocked her head to one side. "I don't see your name on our RSVP list."

"But I called," said Caroline, trying to control the despair in her voice. She had gotten the phone number from Student Services. After the first frustrating conversation with Chrissy, she'd decided not to call her cousin again for information.

Betty smiled. "Come in anyway. Everyone is welcome."

Caroline raised her eyebrows and followed the girl into the house. *Everyone is welcome?* The Sigma Thedas were surprisingly democratic considering their exclusive reputation.

No more than thirty girls were standing in the living room in small groups, conversing quietly. Caroline couldn't help looking down at her silk dress when she saw the others wearing simple blouses and dark skirts. She hadn't meant to overdress. *What's going on*? she had to ask herself. Why is this so different from what I'd imagined?

Things here might not be exactly the way they were back in California. Ellis was from Denver, and she didn't wear white blouses. Caroline hadn't seen a single thing in her roommate's closet that would look out of place in San Francisco or New York. Her own wardrobe was conservative compared to Ellis's clothes.

Betty sat in the center of the cream-colored couch under the front window. "We can get started now that everyone is here. Cecily, please tell the freshman pledges about Alpha Theda."

Cecily folded her hands and began, "As you know, we Alpha Thedas are proud of our contributions to the community. Several times a year we donate money to deserving causes both on campus and in town. We earn money for these charities by serving at alumni dinners and other functions held on campus where we are paid minimum wage."

Alpha Theda! Caroline screamed silently She should have known she was in the wrong place and escaped when she had a chance. All she could think of doing now was finding Chrissy— and killing her without leaving a trail of evidence!

ABOUT THE AUTHOR

Janet Quin-Harkin is the author of more than forty books for young adults, including the best-selling *Ten-Boy Summer* and *On Our Own*, its sequel series. Ms. Quin-Harkin lives just outside of San Francisco with her husband, three teenage daughters, and one son.